ZODIAC LOVERS

Paranormal Romance

Book Two

TAURUS ✶ GEMINI ✶ CANCER

LANCE TAUBOLD

DEDICATION

FOR HEATHER GRAHAM, AN INCREDIBLE AUTHOR AND
EVEN MORE INCREDIBLE FRIEND. THANK YOU FOR ALL
THE GREAT YEARS AND GOOD TIMES AND THE ONES
YET TO COME..

TABLE OF CONTENTS

TAURUS

Taurus—The Bull

Traits: Patient, Reliable, Warm-Hearted, Loving, Persistent, Determined, Jealous, Possessive, Resentful, Inflexible, Security-Loving.

1863 Gettysburg

"Martin, I've been shot."

"I'm here, Johnny. I've got you. You're goin' to be fine." Tears formed in Martin's eyes, as he cradled the head of his best friend and lover in his lap. They sat beneath a chestnut oak, which Martin had managed to get them to after the Union onslaught. He could still hear gunfire in the distance.

"That damn Yankee got me, Martin. The sneaky bastard shot me in the back." Johnny coughed. Blood and spittle drooled from his mouth. I don't think I'm gonna make it." He reached up and grabbed the hand that was stroking his forehead. "Hold me, Martin. Don't ever let me go."

The tears poured down Martin's face. He clutched Johnny to his chest and put his forehead to Johnny's. Martin noticed the coolness of Johnny's forehead, despite the grueling July heat. "I'll never let you go. Johnny, don't leave me. What'll I do without you?" He was sobbing now.

They'd known each other since they were three. Their families were very close and Johnny's older brother, Jacob, and his own sister, Viola, had married two years ago and joined their families together. He had first kissed Johnny when they were thirteen. They'd been together ever since. Their families had never known about them. Even the war hadn't separated them.

They'd enlisted together in Virginia's First Cavalry unit two years ago and had fought side by side ever since, neither ever getting so much as a scratch. They'd become something of a legend in their division.

And now it was all coming to an end.

"I'll wait for you, Martin. I promise. We're destined to be together. You're special." He coughed and choked up blood again. "We're special."

"Yes, we are. And you're the special one," Martin wailed. "I love you so much."

"I know you do, Martin. As much as I love you." His eyes began to flutter and close.

"Don't go, Johnny. Please." Martin's heart was breaking.

"I'll wait for you." Johnny's eyes closed. "Always."

"Yes, wait for me, Johnny. I'll find a way somehow. I'll be with you. Always." Martin could only hold him and cry.

The gunshots came closer. The tree they were leaning against wouldn't provide much cover. He had to get away, but he couldn't leave his love. "I'll be back, Johnny. I promise." Martin leaned over and kissed him one last time. He got up and gently put Johnny's head on the ground. "Nothin'll keep us apart. I'll be back."

Two gray uniformed men ran by a little distance away. He heard a shot and one fell.

The damn Yankees were still coming. He had to get out of there.

But what about Johnny? He looked down at him, heard more shots, and knew he had to run.

As he ran, his thoughts were only of how after this battle he would come back and get Johnny and take him home to the place where they had chosen to be buried together.

He barely felt the shot enter his back and pierce his heart.

Present Day

"Dr. Berger, your three o'clock is here," the intercom's voice sounded. Talon Berger pushed the button atop the intercom. "Thanks, Jeff. Send him in." Talon glanced at his Submariner Rolex. Eight minutes early. He liked punctuality. But he never fussed if patients were late, and also never counted down the time at the end of a patient's session. He didn't want his patients to feel the pressure. He was there to help people. In this regard, he was unlike so many of his fellow psychiatrists who valued the almighty dollar. Consequently, he didn't consort with many of that ilk. He did very well and had a full client list. He wasn't lacking for anything. Well, except a boyfriend. No time to dwell on that. He had a new patient to see. A new challenge. Talon always enjoyed new patients. He loved to hear what story they had to tell.

Talon's patient was Matthew Braun. A good, strong-sounding German name. It sounded familiar. Hmm. Matt Braun. Wasn't that a character in a Western novel series?

The door opened.

Holy shit!

"Hello. Sorry, I'm a little early."

The man who stood in the doorway—or rather, filled the doorway—was about 6' 2", Talon's own height, about thirty-five, his own age—, and about as close to the perfect Aryan German as could be. The Aryans could have used him as a prototype. Very short blond hair, crystal-blue eyes, broad shoulders and chest, narrow hips... well-

4

filled-out slacks. All right, he needed to be professional here. Even though it had been a full year—God, a year—since he'd had sex. His last disaster, Rick (The Fuck), had left him after eight months, which was fine. Talon had been ready to throw him out, the lying, cheating asshole that Rick was.

The Germanic god spoke again, "Is something wrong?"

"Uh, no. Just finishing a thought. Please come in." Talon came from behind his desk to greet the man, proffering his hand. "Talon Berger."

"Matt Braun." He shook Talon's hand in a firm grip. They locked eyes. "Have we met before?"

Talon felt the heat from the man's hand, while he stared back, thinking the same thing. "I don't believe so. But there is something familiar about you. Although, I'm sure I would have remembered meeting someone like you."

"Like me?"

Talon was momentarily mind-blocked. "I meant that I have a good memory for faces." Weak save.

"Oh," was all Matt Braun said.

Talon realized their hands were still locked. He released the man's hand and instantly felt a cool rush over his own.

"You have a firm handshake," Matt said. "I like that. It shows confidence, not bravado. I made a good choice."

"Thank you," Talon responded, slightly disconcerted, and not only by the man's looks. There was something more going on here. If he believed in a sixth sense, he would have said he felt danger. But other than his size, the man was not threatening. The opposite in fact. For all his size and musculature, he seemed convivial and approachable. "Well, Mr. Braun—"

"Matt, please. I've never been comfortable with formality, Talon." He smiled.

Talon smiled back. The majority of his patients called him 'Doc,' or 'Doctor.' He ultimately didn't care, whatever they were comfortable with. None called him 'Talon,' though. Intriguing. The familiarity felt suitable with Matt. Hopefully, this inchoate relationship would continue. There was never a guarantee that the doctor/patient relationship would gel.

"The first session, I like to get to know my patient, get a rapport established, get a feel for your needs, and ascertain if we will continue," Talon told Matt.

"You mean this is a test?" Matt said.

"Not at all. But it has happened in the past that I've felt I wasn't the 'right man for the job,' so to speak, and have recommended another psychiatrist. I like my patients to be open and honest. If there seems to be fear or animosity, I have to take stock and suggest the best alternative."

Matt smiled. "I'll try to keep my animosity toward you to a minimum then."

"A sense of humor. Good start," Talon said, meaning it. "I'll ask you a few questions, and you, in turn, may also ask me some."

"Sounds fair. Do I get to lie on the couch?" Matt tipped his head, gesturing across the room. "It looks comfy."

"It is. I don't usually use it for the first session, and sometimes not at all. It depends on the patient. However, it does make a wonderful nap place for me between patients."

"Ah, so that's why it's comfy. Not so altruistic, eh, Talon?"

"I'm pragmatic." He liked this man. "Please be seated." Talon referenced the chair on the front side of his desk, then proceeded to his own chair opposite Matt. "Why don't you start off telling me a little of your background, etc."

Matt stared at Talon and took a deep breath. "I was born here in Chicago, went to The University of Oklahoma on a football scholarship. I was a tight end for the Sooners. I decided not to pursue football, got my degree at their College of Architecture, came back here about eight years ago, and got a job with Parkman and Sloan. I like it. They like me and my ideas." He paused. "Let's see. What else? I'm thirty-four, gay, had three or four semi-serious relationships, but no one at the moment. I like candle-lit dinners and walks on the shore in the moonlight. I have no communicable diseases. Blue is my favorite color. A good cabernet is my favorite wine. I love pizza, Chicago dogs, vanilla ice cream... Why are you laughing?"

Talon tried to stifle himself, as he removed the hand from his mouth that he'd hoped would hide his mirth. "You do realize you're in a psychiatrist's office and not applying at E-Harmony or Match.com?"

"I know. I'm just nervous. I thought I'd try to be funny. I don't like talking about myself. Sorry," Matt said, sinking back into the chair.

"It's quite all right. You *were* funny, and it did give me some insight to your character. I'm going to take my jacket off, if you don't mind. The laughing has made me warm." Talon stood to put his jacket over the back of his chair. He would normally hang it in his office closet, but he didn't want to take the time right now. Things were rolling along well, and he didn't want to lose momentum. He also enjoyed looking at Matt.

"Please be comfortable," Matt said, sitting up now. "I like that jacket. The gray makes your near-black eyes stand out. You're very handsome, you know."

"Thank you," Talon mumbled, and looked down at his jacket, playing with the collar as if it were rich sable.

"Sorry, again. I'm not flirting. I'm only stating a fact." Matt said, without any apparent mendacity.

"You're very frank, Matt." Talon seated himself again.

"I think it's a defense mechanism. I know I can appear intimidating, so I try to let people know up front what I think. And the more nervous I get, the franker... more frank I get. You're pretty buff for a psychiatrist. You must hit the gym a lot, too."

"I try to go as often as possible." Talon was getting uncomfortable. The conversation had gotten out of hand and become a little *too* familiar. He needed to retake control. And this man was *too* good-looking by half. "A few more questions, Matt, and please relax. There's nothing to be nervous about."

"Okay, I'll try, but I'm already starting to sweat." Matt grabbed the front of his polo shirt and pulled it in and out.

That statement sent Talon's mind in a different direction, one his unquenched libido needed to squelch. Yet there was this underlying, niggling feeling of comfort with this man. "Do you have family here?"

"My parents live in Evanston. My older sister lives in Lansing with her husband and two kids, and a younger brother—not married, but straight—in Green Bay," Matt rattled off.

"Do you get along with them?"

"Oh yeah, we all get along great. My mom wants me to find someone. She's liked them all and says I'm too picky." Matt chuckled. "She says if I'm not careful, I'll be an old maid."

"So they have no issue with your being gay?"

"None at all. I knew—and they did too—when I was in high school." Matt leaned back now, seeming more at ease.

"Did you get any flak or censure from any of your friends or classmates?" Talon was in his milieu now and breathed an inner sigh of relief.

"Not really. I didn't announce it or anything. I even dated a few girls. I didn't do much with them. There were only a couple of guys I messed around with, and they didn't talk. And even in high school I was over six feet and two hundred pounds, which didn't hurt either. Not too many would want to mess with me."

"Yes, intimidating."

Matt winked at him and smiled.

"So, would you say that you had a happy childhood?" Talon was trying to be professional and not respond to the wink and smile.

"Absolutely. Being gay never bothered me. I like it. Guys are great. I like women too, just not in a sexual way. I usually go for muscular guys like me, which may be a little narcissistic, but what can I say. You're the shrink guy, you tell me."

Talon couldn't help but laugh again. This was clearly *not* a typical first interview session.

"I love your laugh. It makes you even more charming. Your whole face lights up. Oh sorry, I think I *might* be flirting a little now." Matt stood up and leaned over on the desk, almost in Talon's face. "Are you gay?"

Talon quickly sobered.

Matt straightened. "Crossed a line? I thought maybe it was my turn to ask a question."

"No, it's all right. I have a couple of more, but why don't you ask yours." Talon mentally prepared himself for the onslaught of what he was sure would be a barrage of personal, intimate questions. He could always stop them, of course, but that wasn't his modus operandi. It might give more insight into Matt's character and, to be frank, he wanted this man to know him. He looked up into Matt's eyes, where he was still looming over the desk. "And, 'yes,' to your first question." *Here we go.*

"Good. That makes me more comfortable already, the kindred spirit thing." Matt sat down. "You can relate better. Are you single?"

"Yes."

"Seeing anyone?"

"No."

"Had many steady relationships?"

"Three or four."

"Ever been in love?"

"I thought so—every time—but no, not in love. There was love, yes, on certain levels. Lust, yes. But not *in* love." Talon felt he hadn't explained that very well.

"Me neither." Matt nodded. "Kindred spirits." He seemed to look through Talon for a moment. "Family?"

"Just an older brother and his family: wife, two sons, eight and nine. They live in Seattle and I visit them at Christmas. I love my nephews and if I ever had children, I would choose them."

"Do you want children?" Matt leaned forward and put clasped hands on the desk. "Can I have a cup of coffee? I've wanted one since I walked in here and smelled it. It smells great."

"Of course, I should have offered." Talon went to the small sideboard against the wall, where the coffee maker was prominently displayed, along with several dark mugs. Talon grabbed one and the coffee pot.

"Black, please," Matt said.

Talon poured, and grabbed another mug for himself. He could use another cup. "I like mine black, too. I'm a purist. I do have the appurtenances for those who decide to destroy one of God's finest creations, but I keep them underneath the counter, in case." He walked to Matt and handed him a mug, then returned to his chair. He eased into the leather, and after raising the mug to his lips and sipping, said, "Ethiopian. Dark. Rich. You can taste the true essence of the bean and the roast. Nothing else is required."

"Very eloquently put, Doc. Of course, I've always thought a touch of brandy never hurt: the true essence of the bean and the roast." Matt chuckled and sipped. "Mmm. This *is* good."

"I'm glad you approve, and I do have to agree with you on the occasional addition of the brandy. Actually, I have some in the cabinet for those occasions. Would you care for a tipple?" Talon started to rise.

"Not now. I'm enjoying this as is. I want to keep a clear head. Matt raised the mug to his lips again. "Rain check, though."

Talon felt a quick rush of excitement at the 'future' promise.

"So. Children?" Matt was leaning forward again.

"Yes, if I found someone to share them with, who was like-minded, someone I truly could rely on, who would always be there. Forever. But there are no guarantees, so probably... no." Talon realized he had never voiced these thoughts before.

"How old are you?"

"Thirty-five, next month."

"Ah, same age. Taurus?"

Talon paused. "Ah, the zodiac. Yes, I'm a Taurus, though I don't take much stock in astrology. You are quite the master of the *non sequitur*. Have you learned enough?"

"Not hardly," Matt said. "But I'll give you a break from my *non sequiturs* for now. I don't want you to think I'm a Torquemada or something."

"Torquemada?" Talon sat back, realizing that he had been leaning on his desk similarly to Matt.

"I like history, mostly American war history, but some European, too. The Spanish Inquisition was fascinating—barbaric—but fascinating." Matt took another healthy sip of coffee.

"Well, Matt, let's get down to your reason for wanting to see me."

"Hmm. Maybe this might be the time for the brandy. You might need one, too." Matt squirmed in his chair, wriggled his shoulders, and wagged his neck from side to side, apparently trying to loosen the tension from his upper body.

Talon gave a look of consternation. "Please, Matt, I've probably heard it before. I've been doing this for years. It's reasonably difficult to surprise me, and remember, I'm on your side. I'm here to help you."

"Promise me you won't tell me I'm crazy—even if you think I am." Matt was clutching the arms of the chair, visibly tense.

"That wouldn't be very professional of me. You have to trust me." Talon felt an unusual fervency in his words... almost a desperation for this man to believe him.

"I want to. I almost feel as if you're the only one who *can* help me." Matt's entire demeanor had changed. The fun-loving, cocky jock had become a lost little boy.

Talon was very disconcerted and could nearly feel the air thickening around them. It was palpable.

"Do you believe in reincarnation?" Matt's look was intense and deadly serious.

"I don't deny the possibility of it. But I don't ascribe to it either. I have read of many documented cases from some very renowned people, including several psychiatrists of note." He'd actually done quite a bit of research into the subject, and had always had an odd affinity for it. It had become something of an avocation, but he didn't feel quite comfortable telling Matt this, and it was a little distressing that he had even broached the topic. "Why do you ask me, Matt?"

Matt's tension eased slightly, and he started speaking. "I've been having these recurring dreams—nightmares. I'm always in a battle of some kind, and I think I always die. They're driving me crazy. They occur most nights now. They used to be sporadic. I don't want to sleep. Sometimes, I wake up screaming... for something, or *for* someone, but I never know what or who it is. Sometimes I wake up crying—like, gut-wrenching sobbing. I feel like if I could just figure out what they mean, or if I could figure out what I'm looking for, they would stop. I need some kind of answer." He put his palms on the desk. "Please, Talon, I *know* you can help me." It was a plea.

Talon knew he would have to try. He felt an odd connection to Matt. "All right, Matt. I will try my best."

"Thank you. I knew my friend was right." Matt put his head down on the desk.

"Your friend?"

"She's actually my secretary, but I also count her as friend. In spite of her trying to match-make for me, she is also very caring. You were recommended through friends of a friend of hers. And she'd also told me she heard you were very cute—which is an understatement—but that's not why I decided to come. I was desperate and prayed you could help." Matt leaned back. "I already feel better. When do we start? Tomorrow?"

Talon hoped he wasn't making a huge mistake as he scrolled through his appointment calendar on his desktop computer. It was completely filled for tomorrow and most of the week. "What time is best for you?"

"Is early evening available? After work? Although, I make my own schedule. Anytime you can squeeze me in, I'll make it work." Matt had excitement in his voice now.

Talon never did evening sessions. He looked at his schedule. "My last appointment is at 4:30. Would 6:00 work?" What was he doing?

"Perfect." Matt clapped his hands together. "We could grab a bite to eat after, since I'm your last appointment." He said it as a statement.

Talon felt himself nod.

"Great. I'll see you at 6:00... or maybe a little before." Matt smiled, stood, turned, and left the office.

Talon stared after the man, shaking his head. *What am I doing?*

* * *

Talon stared at the clock: 5:45. He'd been staring at it for almost an hour. His 4:30 had cancelled. Now he was just waiting for Matt. He'd had a troubled sleep the night before, and his day had not gone much better. He was too distracted with thoughts of Matt and his problem. He had already anticipated potential hypnosis for past-life regression, if indeed, reincarnation was a possibility. He was timorous ... and excited. Reincarnation. Could it be real? Talon had never felt so confounded. Add to that the burgeoning feelings he had for Matt—and only after one meeting. He self-analyzed his obvious lust. The man was certainly perfect looking. There was more here though, something deeper—hidden. He felt driven to discover what it was; he felt desperate to know, almost as if it was his destiny. Matt was obviously interested in him. But that needed to be tempered if he was going to do his job.

A quick rap on the door, and the door opened.

There he was.

Matt.

Or was it? Another figure momentarily stood there, then it dissolved into the handsome Aryan man: a polo shirt again—turquoise—and tight, his nipples prominent; and blue jeans—also

16

tight. Devastating. Where was his coat? Talon cleared his throat. "Come in, Matt. No coat?"

"Thanks. I left it out there." His head cocked back to the reception area. "Nobody before me?"

"They cancelled."

"Nap time for you then?" His head cocked to the couch.

"No. I was catching up on a few things." Talon moved some papers on his desk to verify his statement. "Coffee? I made a fresh pot."

"How thoughtful. Sure." Matt paused. "And a splash of brandy, if that's okay. I need something to calm me a little. I couldn't work all day, thinking about this session. I slept pretty well though. No dreams. See, you're helping me already."

Talon handed him a mug. "I'll stick to the pure stuff." He sipped his own coffee.

"I understand. Maybe later, at dinner?"

Dinner. Talon had half-hoped Matt had forgotten his inadvertent dinner agreement after the session. Perhaps he could beg off. But did he want to?

"Let's start with your telling me your dreams, or at least as much as you can remember."

"Oh, I can remember them pretty well. I'm always in battle, in some war."

"Some war?"

"Yeah. The Civil War. World War II. Vietnam. Those are the only ones. And I'm not even that knowledgeable about Vietnam. It's not my favorite era, nor America's most shining moment. So much ugliness and deceit. Not that war is pretty, but Vietnam was more savage and inhumane. It seemed to bring out the worst in man, at least that's my opinion." Matt finished his coffee. "Can I have some more? Maybe a little more brandy, too. I'm so tense."

"Of course." Talon got up to get the drink. "You're perfectly safe here. I want you to feel comfortable."

"Oh, I feel comfortable with you. Maybe too much. I think I came on a little strong yesterday, but I felt like I could talk to you and be honest. If I get out of hand again, just smack me or tell me to shut the fuck up or something. Sorry, I didn't mean to curse."

"Please, don't temper your speech. I encourage frankness in my patients. If they feel they have to mitigate their speech or thoughts, they will not be as apt to be forthright or honest. So, curse away. I've been known to indulge myself now and then." Truth be told, Talon could hold his own with any stevedore, as evidenced by some of his past verbal sparring with Rick. "My last boyfriend and I got into quite a few curse-up-a-blue-streak bouts. I usually won." Why had he told Matt that?

"I would have bet on you hands down with your vocabulary." Matt nodded.

"I hope I don't come off pompous. I enjoy words. I'm not trying to show off." Talon's face showed concern.

"Not at all. It's cute. When I need your unabridged Oxford, though, I'll ask you to pull it out." Matt smiled, ingenuously.

Talon returned the smile, liking the easy camaraderie. Rick had always given him shit about his verbal prowess. "Let's get back to your dreams."

Matt took a large gulp of the spiked coffee before replying, "Can't we just get to the hypnosis thing. Somehow I *know* that's what'll help. I feel it. Please." That desperation again. "Talon. Please." This time, almost deadpan, his eyes locked on Talon's.

Talon felt himself nodding. "All right. I've never done this at a first session. I can't guarantee any success. Usually, a patient needs to feel comfortable and relaxed. They can feel awkward or be resistant at going under."

"I'm very comfortable with you, as I said. Also, I meditate. I learned in college. I used to do it before games. It would get me centered and focused. A boyfriend, our quarterback actually, got me into it... as well as lot of other things." Matt gave a lasciviously playful wink. "But it did really help, and I still do it several times a week. So, putting me under will be a snap."

Talon was still hesitant, but nodded again as he thought about the "things" Matt and his quarterback had gotten into. He cleared his throat. "Well then, want to try out my comfy couch?"

"Absolutely." Matt gave that lascivious wink again, got up, and walked over to the couch. "You don't mind if I slip my shoes off? I feel more comfortable and I don't want to scuff up your couch."

"That's fine." Talon watched him slip the loafers off and unceremoniously plop himself down."

"This *is* comfy." Matt patted the cushions. "It would be great for more than just naps."

Talon's eyes widened slightly, and his thoughts instantly pictured Matt naked and willing.

"I meant sleeping. Of course, it would be good for *that*, too." Matt smiled, then adjusted his position the couch, moving a pillow behind his head.

Talon felt his face redden. The man had read his facial inference. No way out of that one. Ignore and move on. "Are you comfortable?"

"Yes."

"I'm going to take you through a series of color levels to focus your concentration. I want you to home in on the sound of my voice and picture what I describe to you," Talon began.

"I can do that. My own meditation involves images, too." Matt closed his eyes. "Be gentle, Doc." Matt smiled, eyes still closed.

Talon grinned. "I'll try. I want you to picture a blue sky. Pure blue. No clouds. Just a serene blue. Everywhere you look, nothing but sky blue. Can you see it?"

"Yes. I'm there." Matt's breathing was already even. Body totally relaxed. He was good at this.

"Focus on the sound of my voice. Breathe slowly and deeply. In. Out. That's good. Now, we're moving up in the sky. It's changing to green. Kelly green. A rich, bright green." Talon watched Matt relax even more as his head fell back, exposing more of his neck. "The sky is changing again. Now it's becoming orange. A deep orange, like the most perfect, succulent orange you've ever seen. Keep focusing on my voice. When I say "wake up," you will instantly awaken, feeling refreshed. You will remember everything. Do you understand?"

Matt's jaw relaxed and his mouth fell open an inch. "Yes... Martin."

Talon jerked back in the chair he had placed at Matt's side. Martin?

Matt's body started to squirm, then jerked.

Talon watched the odd movement. Matt seemed to have been poked by something in the back.

Talon continued, "Just listen to my voice and—"

"Martin, hold me. I love you. Don't leave me. *Please don't leave me. I'm so scared.*"

Talon responded almost involuntarily, "I'm here. Don't be afraid." He'd never seen this before—never seen such a quick response. Perhaps Matt was faking this. Maybe he was being duped.

"No, Martin! Hold me!" It was a scream this time.

Talon couldn't help himself. The scream was so desperate. There was no way Matt was faking this. Talon moved onto the couch. He clutched the man to his chest; Matt clutched back. Tears ran down his face.

"I don't want to die, Martin. I don't want to leave you. It hurts so much."

"You're not going to die. You'll be fine." Talon didn't know how else to respond. Matt's hold was almost a death-grip.

"I know I *am*, Martin. Please tell me I'm your Johnny. Tell me you love me. Tell me we'll be together forever. *Please*, Martin. I want to hear it one last time."

Matt's grip weakened, losing strength. Dying? This couldn't be a farce. It was too real. He felt himself saying, "You're my Johnny. I love you. We'll be together forever."

"I trust you, Martin. I know we will."

Matt's grip loosened and his head lolled on Talon's chest.

What was happening?

He couldn't be dead. It wasn't possible.

"Wake up. Wake up, Matt."

Nothing.

Talon shook him. "Wake up!"

Blue eyes fluttered open. "This feels nice." Matt clutched the arms embracing him.

"Are you all right?"

"Yeah, I'm fine. Pretty crazy, huh?"

"You're not crazy, Matt." Talon hesitated a moment to collect his thoughts. "Do you remember everything?"

"Oh yeah. It's one of the same dreams I always have.

"Can you tell more about it?" Talon started to feel uneasy. "Where was this?"

"On the battlefield in the Civil War. I'd been shot, and I think, dying in my lover's arms. Martin's his name." He scrutinized Talon's face. "I'm not making this up. And I'm not being cavalier about it. I'm trying to be calm on the outside so I don't explode from what I'm feeling on the inside. I'm really lost. Do you have any idea of what's happening here? Is it reincarnation? It feels so real for me—this, and the other dreams. It's me experiencing this. I *know* it is.

"I'm not sure what's happening here, yet. And I don't want to give you some gobbledygook just to placate you. I respect your intelligence too much. It's a process, and I won't tell you that this might not take some time, or that it will be easy. But we will find out what's happening here. I promise you." Talon said this last as much of confirmation to Matt as to himself.

"Thank you, Talon." He squeezed Talon's arms tightly. "I know you will."

Such sincerity and vulnerability... and trust came from this big man that Talon wasn't sure if he was up to the task. All he knew, at the moment, was that he *must* try to help. Much more was going on here than he could readily assimilate. He now became aware that Matt was still in his arms... and apparently not doing anything to extricate himself. Talon knew he had to make the first move—in spite of the satisfying naturalness at being so intimate with this man. "Matt, you can sit up now, if you're feeling all right that is"

"I feel surprisingly fine. And comfortable. You feel good." Matt hugged Talon's arms once more, before adding, "It feels natural, like we've done this before."

Talon didn't want to acknowledge the veracity of the statement, so instead removed his arms and pushed Matt to a sitting position. "I think that's enough for today." What had he just witnessed?

"Okay. I'm hungry anyway. I do feel better though, as if something has been released from me. I'm sure you've helped me already, Talon. Do you like barbecue?"

Talon should have been used to the non-sequiturs by now, but the barbecue threw him. He needed time to think, but he didn't want to leave Matt. The man had, moments ago, been screaming in his arms, and now he was talking about barbecue. It didn't add up. "Barbecue sounds great. I need to change, however. I have some more casual clothes here. One stipulation though." Talon paused and Matt regarded him with a look of askance. "We will not discuss this session until your next appointment. I need time to process this and to decide a possible recourse."

"Done. I'm sure we can find other topics of conversation. I really want to know all about you." Matt smiled warmly.

"I'll just be a moment," Talon replied, moving toward his office bathroom. He sat on the commode and shook his head. What had made him give in to Matt's request for hypnosis? He'd never done that before. He was a professional for God's sake. And he hadn't even regressed him. Matt had gone straight into a... memory? Dream? Fantasy? He couldn't figure it out. Next time he would have to be more careful. Next time...

Yes, he knew it wouldn't and couldn't end here. He was part of this merry-go-round of events. He knew it. This was going somewhere beyond his own encounters. He needed to be there for its unfolding. But what would dinner be like?

Dinner was pleasant, the conversation fast and interesting. And if Talon didn't glean any more insight into Matt's problem, it was all right. He'd learned more about the man, and he'd liked what he'd learned. Somewhere along the way, he'd committed himself. He eschewed the unwritten rule of getting involved with a patient and pushed forward. It felt right. Of course, this wasn't something he'd share this with any of his colleagues. But screw it. It was his life, and if he thought he could make it better, he was going to try. Nothing was prosaic about this situation or this man.

They stood in the parking lot next to Matt's car. Matt leaned against the car door. "Can we do this the same time tomorrow?"

Talon had instantly said yes.

"Dinner, too?"

"I have to eat, right?"

"Absolutely." Matt grinned, leaned into Talon, and gave him a quick kiss on the lips, before he jumped into his midnight-blue Mercedes and drove off.

That abrupt kiss sealed the deal for Talon. Any possible regrets he'd had over dating—yes, dating—a patient were obliterated with that soft brush of a kiss on his lips. A tingle, almost a shock from the contact, yet a familiarity at the same time had said: This is right. In his interpretation. He wasn't going to psychoanalyze himself. It would only drive him crazy. "Let's see where you lead me, Matt Braun," Talon voiced to the receding Mercedes.

✳ ✳ ✳

"Bobby, I know the 4th Marines are the best, and I'm right glad we're part of them, but do you think Colonel Howard was just giving us a load of bull when he said them Japs would never take Malinta Tunnel. I mean, we're still using these old World War I grenades. Them Japs have got them knee mortars. And sure, yesterday we whupped them up by North Point, but they just keep comin', like rats or somethin'. When're the reinforcements supposed to show up? An' while you're at it, tell me why MacArthur high-tailed it outta here a few months ago? Did he know somethin' Genr'l Wainright don't? I know I'm ramblin', but, Bobby, it's your birthday and I wanted it to be kinda special for you—besides last night 'a course. I know, you said your birthday ain't till tomorrow, but it's May sixth here today. Ya know, I don't get that whole international dateline-time-thing. I just know I love you, and I want today to be somethin' special. And are you hot? It's hotter 'n hell in this tunnel. I hope we ain't here long. I bet back home it's nice. Springtime. Not this sweat box."

"You finished?" Bobby's teeth gleamed bright in contrast to the dark tan he'd acquired after days spent guarding the beach. His hair had also bleached out, becoming almost platinum blonde. Chip loved his hair and had stroked it endlessly after they'd made love on a secluded part of the beach last night at midnight to celebrate his birthday. Occasionally, over the last few months they'd been here, they'd managed to slip away to be together. A couple of their buddies who knew about them had covered for them.

Chip and he did their jobs and did them well, that was all anyone cared about. Sex between two guys... well they weren't the only ones. But... they were the only ones in love.

Chip and he had been together for three years now—almost since they'd enlisted and Bobby had walked into the barracks at boot camp. He'd walked in the door and seen the short, muscular, cute-as-a-button, Texas cowboy, naked as the day he was born, hootin' an' hollerin' and waving a towel around like a lariat. Chip had stopped waving when he spotted him, dropped the towel on the floor, walked right over to him, held out his hand, and said, "Howdy, I'm Chip. An' I'm the best damn cowboy and the best damn Marine you're ever gonna meet." And it was true. He'd fallen for him then and there.

Now, this is where their journey had brought them. Corregidor. Funny name. No wonder they called it "The Rock," but the weather was beautiful here, and it wasn't any more peculiar a name than Punxsutawney, Pennsylvania, his hometown, and home to the famous Phil the groundhog.

Hopefully, they wouldn't be here much longer and this damn war would end so they could go home and start their lives together in Montana. That's where they'd decided to live—away from folks and their mis-notions about them, where Chip could ride, and they'd buy a ranch with the money his folks had left after they'd both passed from the fire that had destroyed so many homes in his neighborhood. He choked up thinking about his beloved parents. He wished they could have met Chip. They would have loved him. Everybody loved him. He was a great, fun-loving guy and a helluva Marine. But nobody loved him as much as he did... or ever would. He'd promised Chip they would always be together, and he would do everything in his power to keep that promise and make sure Chip was safe.

He smiled at Chip. "Now which question did you want me to answer f—"

BOOM!

27

Everything went black.

Bobby was on the ground covered in rocks and rubble.

There was nothing but dust and darkness.

The tunnel must've collapsed, Bobby guessed as he coughed and stirred, slowly moving his limbs.

His brain tried to configure and assimilate, surmising that the Japs must be trying to close off the north entrance, leaving the only way out, the main tunnel.

Bobby rose slowly, groping around him, trying to stand.

Where was Chip?

He began to panic and call frantically. "Chip! Chip! Where are you? Are you all right? Chip! Chip!"

He waited in silence.

Then he began to hear the sounds. Slow moans. Gasps. Grunts. Indistinguishable words.

He waited desperately for the only voice he needed to hear.

Nothing.

The sounds diminished. The gasps and groans dwindled, as he imagined the life exiting from each of his companions in arms.

It was horrific.

Was Chip one of them?

Please God, no. Not my Chip.

Then, very faintly...

"Bobby?"

It was off to his right.

"Chip! Chip I'm here." He scrabbled on his hands and knees to his right, heedless of the rocks and rubble.

"Bobby?" The voice sounded close, if faint.

"Chip, I'm coming. Just wait for me. Don't move."

He scrambled faster toward the sound. He heard a grunt as he hit a blockage.

"Bobby, is that you?"

"I'm here, Chip." He stuck his hand out and met flesh. An arm. His slid his hand down the arm and met fingers. Those familiar fingers that had touched every part of his body and had given him so much pleasure. Now they felt rough and wet. Blood probably. He didn't care. He grasped that hand in his own. With his left hand, he carefully traced a route up Chip's arm to his head. He felt his chin. His cheek. His hair.

Faintly, he heard, "This is bad, Bobby, ain't it? I can't hardly breathe. This is it, huh? I wish I could see your handsome face once more. You're so dang handsome."

Silence.

"Chip! Chip, don't leave me. I'll get help. We'll get out of here. You just hang on."

"It's all right, Bobby. Don't cry." He coughed. "I want you to hold me while I die. That's all I want. You're all I want." Another cough.

"No Chip, you're not dyin' on me. I can't run a ranch without my little cowboy." He sniffled and wanted to wipe away his tears, but couldn't bear to lose contact. He knew he had to try to get help. Chip was covered in rubble, but he couldn't risk moving him and injuring him more. He wished he could see. Which way was out?

""Hold on to me, Bobby. Promise me you won't leave." The voice was getting fainter by the second. "Sing your song for me, Bobby. Your Marine

Hymn. I love that last part about the skivvies... Please, Bobby. I wanna hear it once more."

Bobby's choked voice started,

"First to jump for holes and tunnels

"And to keep our skivvies clean

"We are proud to claim the title

"Of Corregidor's Marines."

He ended on a sob. "I won't leave you, Chip. Not ever. I've got to get some help. Hold on. Trust me." He let go of Chip's hand and started off in what he hoped was the right direction.

"No, Bobby. Please. Don't leave me."

"I'll be right—"

BOOM!

Silence.

* * *

Talon woke with a start.

What the fuck was that?

He was covered in sweat; his pillow was soggy; the sheets were drenched. He threw back the top sheet. The rush of air immediately chilled his naked body. He hugged his arms and rubbed the slickness, trying to bring some warmth and comfort to himself. He groped for the bedside light. His eyes blinked pervasively for several seconds as he tried to adapt to the intrusion, noticing also his rapid breathing.

Now, he said aloud, "What the fuck was that?"

He looked for the clock. It should have been on his nightstand. He glanced down at the floor. There it was, pulsing the time. 4:04. He must have knocked it off the table.

He was shivering. The heat was on. It was still March, not exactly shorts weather in Chicago, but he always slept naked. Besides, the chill wasn't only from his sweaty body. His dream was disturbing, to say the least.

He should change the sheets, but it was late and he just didn't feel like it. He rolled to the other side of the bed. He'd have to sleep on the other side tonight. It was not his preferred side of the bed. It had been Rick's. Well, it was time to get rid of that memory too, he decided. He flopped down and drew the covers over him. He smiled smugly, as the arms of Morpheus enfolded him.

$$* * *$$

That afternoon, Talon sat in his office—waiting, staring at nothing. He thought about his dream. He thought about Matt.

The door opened.

"Hi, Handsome. Ready for the craziness to begin?" Matt's head poked around the edge of Talon's office door.

Talon looked up with a smile. "Punctual, as ever."

"I've actually been out there waiting since 5:30," Matt said, contritely. "But I didn't want you to think I was too anxious." He stepped into the room wearing brown slacks and a cream-colored sweater.

Talon took in the man, silently approving the sartorial choice and deciding that Matt could wear a Hazmat suit and have people swooning.

"You could have knocked. My 5:00 cancelled again. I think she needs more help than I can give her."

"Well, if *you* can't help her, she must really be fucked up." Matt laughed. "Sorry, that was out of line. I have no room to talk. I don't think anyone could be more fucked up than I am."

Talon saw a dark wave cross the handsome Germanic features. "Don't worry, Matt. We'll figure this out. I promise." What had he said? He never promised help. That wasn't only incompetent, it was stupid. Trouble. Trouble. Trouble. "Sit down. The requisite coffee?"

"No thanks." Matt slowly shook his head, the consternation still on his face. "Can we just get to it? I had one of the other dreams last night."

Talon hesitated a moment, a prescient thought manifesting. "If that's what you'd prefer, I personally sug—"

"No," Matt snapped abruptly. "I need to get this done." A switch flipped. "Hey Doc, I'm sorry. I don't know what's come over me. This is so unlike me. We'll do whatever you think's best. I can be an asshole sometimes." Matt flopped on the couch. "Actually, how about a shot of your brandy? I need to settle down. The dream last night was more intense than ever. My whole day was wrecked. When

I wasn't thinking about the dream, I was thinking about you and worrying that you thought I was the biggest jerk or lunatic you'd ever met. And I don't think I could handle that right now. I really like you, Talon. I want you to like me. Me," he iterated, his voice catching slightly. "Now, here I am acting like the jerk and looney I was worried you'd think I was. *Shit.* What's wrong with me?"

Talon's heart clutched. What was this man doing to him? He found himself saying, "I do like you, Matt. You needn't worry on that count." He moved to Matt and grabbed his shoulder in assurance. "And we psych types shy away from using vernacular like looney."

Matt covered Talon's hand with his. "Right. Then, I'm good. I can do this." He lay down, then sprang back up, took off his shoes, and grabbed Talon's hand. "One more question."

Talon looked at him. "Was it okay that I kissed you last night? It felt right. You have nice lips. Soft. Sexy. And all I could think about after I did it was doing it again... but for a longer time."

Talon felt heat rise in his face. "Yes, it was okay." He stopped himself from volunteering any more, or telling him he'd had similar thoughts.

"Good. That's a load off my mind." He flopped back down. "Let's do it."

Talon pulled a chair over to the couch and began. "Listen to the sound of my voice. Only my voice. Focus on it. You picture blue—sky blue. Hear my voice. When I say, 'wake up,' you will awaken and be refreshed and remember everything. Blue. Sky blue."

Matt was out. *Amazing.* Talon asked, "Where are you, Matt? What do you see?"

Matt's body seemed to shift inwardly, almost as if he were shrinking, becoming smaller. It wasn't possible. Then—

"*Damnation,* Bobby. Who's Matt? Tell me you're not fuckin' some other cowboy. I'll blow his head off—and his dick *too.* That'd be a good use for those shitty grenades we have. Come on, it's your birthday. Didn't we just have the best darn sex ever? I heard you screamin' my name. *Chip! Chip!* Thank the Lord we're on the beach. Although, the way you were carryin' on, I think the whole 4th heard ya'. Who's Matt? Tell me, or you'll never get my mouth there again."

Talon was in total shock. His mouth hung open. Speechless.

It couldn't be.

His dream.

The beach.

Grenades.

Chip.

He was scared.

"Bobby, I mean it. Who is he?" Matt's hand snaked out and grabbed Talon in the crotch. "Tell me."

Talon gasped. He wasn't in pain. Yet. But the grip was firm. Matt's eyes were closed. He appeared to be totally out. He grabbed Matt's wrist... and was rewarded with more pressure to his genitals. He gasped again.

"Tell me or I'll rip it off."

Talon found his voice. "I... I said 'man'." He hesitated. "I said 'man' not 'Matt',... Chip."

"Aooh. Ain't I the fool, Bobby. You know how jealous I get. I mean, all them guys around here, right? I love you so much, Bobby. I couldn't live without y—"

Matt jerked violently. His hand yanked from Talon's crotch. He curled into a fetal ball. "Bobby?" The voice weak now. "Bobby?"

Talon tried to keep from shaking. He put his hand on Matt's shoulder. "I'm here, Chip."

Hadn't he said those words in his dream?

"I can't hardly breathe. This is it, huh? It's all right, Bobby. Don't cry?" He coughed.

Talon felt the tears on his cheeks. How?

"I just want you to hold me while I die. That's all I want. You're all I want." Another cough.

Talon knew the response. His mouth opened and the words issued forth.

"No, Chip, you're not dyin' on me. I can't run a ranch without my little cowboy."

"Hold onto me, Bobby. Promise me you won't leave." He coughed. "Sing your song for me, Bobby. Your Marine Hymn. I like that last part about the skivvies. Please, Bobby. I wanna hear it once more."

Talon clutched him. He opened his mouth and slowly sang:

"First to jump for holes and tunnels

"And to keep our skivvies clean

"We are proud to claim the title

"Of Corregidor's Marines."

"I won't leave you, Chip. Not ever."

Matt's body relaxed.

Talon came out of his own trance-like state. "Matt. Matt! Wake up. Wake up!"

Nothing. No movement. Talon shook him hard. "Wake up! Matt. *Matt.*" Another shake. "Wake up!"

A flutter of eyelids.

Blue eyes stared up into Talon's. He let out the breath he hadn't realized he'd been holding. An unseen force seemed to guide his head. He bent over and pressed his mouth to Matt's.

Matt's response was immediate. He opened his mouth to Talon's and they began to kiss with an intense, wanton urgency. Their tongues melded in a conflagration of desire—a desire beyond want or need. Beyond lust. It was a fulfillment.

Talon felt his shirt being adroitly removed and thrown behind him, in spite of there being hardly any room for the two of them on his couch. He slid his hands under Matt's sweater, and just as adroitly, slid it up and off over his head. He needed his heated flesh to make contact with Matt's.

They both gasped into each other's mouths as their naked, hairless chests met. They froze, savoring the feeling of their solid flesh meeting each other.

Matt broke the freeze and pulled Talon on top of him. They kissed ardently, as his hands explored and kneaded Talon's defined muscular back.

Talon, now with arms extended upward on either side of Matt's head, pinning it in place with his biceps framing him, devoured Matt's mouth.

Matt's hands slid downward, pulling Talon's hips into his own, their erections moving against one another.

They continued their erotic teasing, as Talon slowly maneuvered Matt to the floor, Matt's weight pressing into him, their simultaneous grunts of passion further enhancing their need.

Talon's concupiscence became primal in his desperation to remove the last vestiges of their clothing—an insane, inexplicable mission to join them, completely unfettered and unencumbered. To be naked, in the purest sense of the word. To become one. To find the ultimate Nirvana—the point of pleasure that words can no longer explain—nor have need to.

The joining of the perfect.

Their bodies came together. Naked flesh to naked flesh. Both bodies so heated they almost combusted—melting into one another. Sweat beaded on their chests and arms as they glided over one another's bodies, hands sliding over taut muscles, exploring the uncharted.

Talon had never felt such perfect musculature on a man. Matt's smooth, inherently Germanic hairless chest, merging with his own chest, also hairless, but not so inherently. Two smooth naked torsos amalgamating.

He wanted to explore Matt's body forever, and Matt apparently wanted to do the same. His hands brought sensations to him that Talon hadn't even known were possible to experience.

They rolled and writhed on the plush carpet, which could never begin to feel as exquisite as the plushness of one another.

Talon marveled at the sensations he caused and received, his body sensitized to Matt's on an ethereal level.

Seamlessly, the oral exploration began. Tongues and teeth enhanced and replaced hands, taking them down new roads of sensual bliss. They stroked and licked. Sucked and bit. Each act moved them toward an ultimate goal—a goal he knew was ineluctable and would change them both forever.

Neither was dominant; neither was submissive. Neither could tell where one ended and the other began. It didn't matter. Nothing was awkward or taboo.

Talon's hands and mouth memorized and embedded the sensations he gave and received. He was in awe over the way Matt knew exactly what pleased him most. And conversely, he knew immanently what pleased Matt most.

As if he had done this before.

Afterward, Talon could never say how they were joined in climax, only that it was simultaneous and right. A double orgasm that transcended definition—a freeing and a bonding.

A paradox of perfection.

* * *

Talon slowly came back to reality.

"Even your sweat smells good," Matt muttered and nuzzled as he kissed him there, then removed his face from Talon's armpit, where he had apparently ended up in their post-coital aftermath.

"I *knew* it was you from the moment I walked in your office." Matt sniffed Talon in affirmation.

Talon remained silent and pulled his arms into his chest.

"Talon?" Matt couldn't keep the anxiety out of his voice.

"No. I shouldn't have done this. This is wrong." Talon extricated himself out from under Matt's leg, which covered his own, and rolled away, leaving Matt to stare at his naked backside.

Talon wanted to stand and remove himself from the situation, but was at odds with himself because of his sustained erection, which he feared would never go away in Matt's presence. And now that he thought about it, he realized that whenever Matt was near, he was never totally flaccid. The man was walking Viagra.

"Talon?"

The questioning, almost melancholy, tone beveled into Talon's heart.

Talon tried for neutral. "Please. Don't say anything." He felt the stare penetrating his back and soul. His body involuntarily flexed away. "Please," he repeated more ardently, "Just go." He hoped Matt didn't hear the slight break of his voice at the end.

Silence.

"All right."

Talon heard the rustling of Matt gathering his clothes, dressing—then, silence again.

Talon hadn't moved. He could feel Matt's eyes boring into him.

"I'll call you," Matt uttered.

Talon flinched at the sound.

A whisper as the door closed, "I love you."

Talon began to cry.

* * *

It was several minutes, maybe an hour, before Talon could reconcile himself to stand up and dress. His mind was still awhirl, trying to comprehend the frightening realization of this impossible implausibility. He needed a drink.

He went to the bar and poured himself a few fingers of brandy. He took a long pull, feeling the slight burn and the heat as it seared his esophagus, then the flush of warmth to his face. He sighed.

Reincarnation. He was reincarnated. And to paraphrase his favorite detective, the master sleuth Sherlock Holmes, 'When you've exhausted all the possibilities the one remaining one must be the truth.'

"I don't think even opium could get me through this one, Watson," he said to the air and took another pull of brandy.

But how could it be? He didn't remember being in the Civil War. But thinking back now, there were hints of the familiar in some of the things Matt had said during his first regression.

Matt. He'd hurt the man. Talon recalled vividly the pain in Matt's voice when he'd said, "I love you." It was palpable. It had torn into Talon's heart.

The sex had been the best he'd ever had. Transcendent. Talon smiled ruefully to himself, thinking, *at least in this lifetime.*

He needed to consider the possibilities. This man was his destiny, and he had to admit the option could not have been a finer one. He had to know more though.

Vietnam. Matt had said there was a Vietnam dream. Another ill-fated one? Were they these star-crossed, war-torn lovers, destined to repeat their fate? Was this his chance to make everything right? There was no chance now of either of them going off to war in this incarnation. Afghanistan was just about finished and both of them were a little old to enlist.

What was he supposed to do? How was he meant to rectify things?

"Ahh!" Talon screamed to his empty office.

Talon glanced to the couch and the carpet, instantly recalling every second of the crazed passion there. As he finished off the liquor, he noticed something under the front of the couch. Underwear. Matt had left it in his haste to leave. Intentionally? He

41

picked the white briefs up and held them to his chest. He immediately felt a stirring in his loins. This was crazy. He had to call him. He had to sort this befuddled insanity out.

Vietnam. He needed to know that story. Maybe the answers lay there.

He went to the desk and grabbed the phone. White briefs in his left hand, he grabbed the phone handle, as he punched the digits with his right.

Ringing. Ringing. Talon caught a faint whiff of Matt from his left hand.

"Hi, this is Matt. Do the requisite and I'll call you back."

Talon's heart jerked at the sound of Matt's voice. "Matt, I'm sorry I was so cold. Things are confusing. I need to see you as soon as possible." He hoped he didn't sound too desperate. "We'll work this out. I promise. Please call me... or come back to the office. I'll be here waiting for you." *That was desperate. 'I promise?' How could I say that? I am desperate.*

Talon put down the phone and the briefs and sat at his desk. He stared at Matt's underwear, lost in thought, ping-ponging between their love-making and trying to recall a century of buried memories.

"Is my underwear that fascinating? I would've left a hankie, but I was fresh out."

Matt.

Talon's head jerked up. A wealth of emotions coursed through him. He rushed to Matt and held him—held him as if he hadn't seen him in years.

They embraced for a while. No words spoken. No words needed.

Talon said, "How...?"

"I only walked around the block a couple of times," Matt responded. "I knew you needed some time. And I hoped it wouldn't be too long. I didn't have a jacket and it still gets cold at night. No Chicago spring yet." Matt looked into Talon's eyes. "Are you all right?"

"I honestly don't know," Talon ventured. "This is uncharted territory. I need answers... answers to so many questions."

Matt tried to pull away.

Talon held him firm, until their eyes locked. "But not about how I feel about you."

Matt relaxed back into Talon's arms, saying, "I can handle that. We can go from there."

"How are you so nonchalant and accepting?" Talon asked.

"Because I knew after our first regression that you were what I'd been searching for. All the answers were you. Everything felt right. I could stop searching." Matt looked again into Talon's eyes. "You can, too." He paused. "Martin... Bobby."

Talon was stoic as the realization hit home. He *was* those men... and more.

"I need to know about Vietnam. Please. I have to find out what happened there." Talon took a breath. "I need all the answers."

"I know you do," Matt said, nodding with a sagacity that belied his years. "Whatever you want, Talon. Now?"

"If you feel up to it."

"I'm up for anything with you, Talon." He thrust his hips into Talon's to confirm his statement.

Talon felt his heat rise, realizing Matt's briefs were still on his desk, and that minimal material separated them. At that moment Talon wanted nothing more than to remove that minimal material. "Your briefs are on my desk if you want them," his voice acquiring a husky tone.

"Maybe later. Let's get to it." Matt, in his own unpredictable way, changed the subject and mood, and stepping back from Talon, went to the couch, adjusting himself in the process.

Talon did the same as he shook his head in befuddlement and joined Matt at the couch.

"Don't be afraid, Talon. It's our destiny," Matt smiled with the warmth of love in his eyes.

Talon returned the smile and said, wryly, "Thanks for the reassurance."

"No problem., Doc. Ready?" He grabbed Talon's hand. "Come with me, into my dream... our dream. I love you."

Talon responded, feeling the deep truth of Matt's words as he said, "I love you, too.

Matt squeezed his hand harder, and if it were possible, reflected his love more fervently.

"Now, close your eyes..." Talon said, wondering if he could join Matt in his dream, and what would be the consequences.

Matt closed his eyes, and as he did so, Talon found himself doing the same.

* * *

"Chad, if we're fighting for South Vietnam, what the hell are we doing in this god-forsaken shit hole in Cambodia? And what kind of friggin' name is Snuol? They shoulda called it 'sewer.' It smells like shit, and it's muggier than the Everglades in August!" the sandy-haired young man said, querulously.

"Mickey, stop whining," Chad said, hitting him in the butt with the rifle. "And watch where you're going. The Cong have all sorts of nasty traps laid throughout the jungle. They're ruthless. You step on one 'a them mines and it'll blow your dick off, and then I won't want you anymore."

"Aw, Chad, you'd still love me wouldncha? You said I'm the cutest guy in the whole platoon, and the best kisser you ever had."

"Yeah, but we're only twenty-years-old, and I'm not gonna spend the rest of my life with a guy with no dick, no matter how cute you are. Priorities, ya know." Chad faked a rifle tap to Mickey's crotch.

"Hey, watch it. You might need that later." Mickey laughed and ran a few paces ahead, sneaking behind a tree. "Chad, come here, quick."

Chad hustled to join him. "What is it?"

Mickey grabbed Chad's head and pulled it to him, kissing him hard. "I'm glad we were numbers twenty one and twenty two in the lottery. If not for this friggin' war, I never woulda met you. See, somethin' good's come from it." He kissed him again. "I love you."

"I love you, too, you brat. But come on, the guys're right behind us." Chad grabbed Mickey's hand and pulled him back onto the path.

"They all probably know anyway. You get kinda loud sometimes." Mickey chuckled. *"It's cute... like you. And a real turn on."*

"Shut up. I'm not that loud."

"If you say so." Then Mickey lowered his voice. *"Chad?"*

"Now what?"

"Are we really gonna be together forever—like you said?"

"Mickey, how many times I gotta tell you. I'll be here as long as you want me. 'Cuz I'll always want you. You and me. Forever." Chad glanced back, then planted a quick kiss on Chad's lips. *"Now, let's concentrate on making it through this shit storm. We've got R 'n' R in a couple of weeks. I was thinkin' Australia might be fun."*

"Yeah, Australia. Sounds perfect." Chad grinned. *"I sure hope the ARVN know what they're doing with this 'luring the tiger down the mountain' tactic. I mean, what kinda Oriental mystic shit is that? We been tryin' to lure the Cong out, but they keep runnin' away. Sneaky, cowardly bastards, layin' all these crazy traps and mines. Guerilla warfare my ass. Even gorillas are more human than they are. It's not right, Chad, ya know. And I hate bein' on point. It's like we're sittin' guinea pigs."*

"Ducks. Mickey Mouse."

"Don't call me that. I hate Mickey Mouse. He's got that whiney voice and those..."

"Ahhh!"

The ground gave way beneath them. Chad grabbed for Mickey, enfolding him as they fell ten feet down...

And onto a bed of sharpened spikes.

"Chad?" the pain-filled, teary voice burbled.

"I've got you, Mickey. I'm here."

"God, it hurts so much." Mickey tried vainly to get closer to Chad, the
spikes preventing much movement.

"It'll stop soon, Mickey. I won't let you go." The blood streamed from
his mouth as he tried to comfort his lover. "Close your eyes, Mick. Think about
Australia, the beach, the ocean. Just the two of us. Forever."

* * *

Jeff, Talon's office assistant, arrived early, as he did every
morning. He knew Talon liked his coffee ready and waiting, and he
made sure that Talon's desk was always neat and organized. He loved
working for him. Besides the fact that Talon was a *twelve* in the looks
department, he was also a great guy.

He opened the door to Talon's office. The desk was directly
ahead, and Jeff immediately noticed what appeared to be a pair of
white briefs in the middle of it.

He moved toward the desk, then jerked to the right, catching
sight of the two men entwined on the couch, both fully clothed, and
apparently sleeping. Talon was one. He didn't recognize the blond
man with him. *Guess Talon got lucky.*

Something struck him as odd, though. Unnatural.

"Talon?" he whispered.

Then a little louder. "Talon? I didn't mean to intrude."

He moved closer, a dire feeling burgeoning. Neither man
appeared to be breathing. They were locked together, unmoving.

Jeff froze. Should he call the police? An ambulance?

He had to be sure. He slowly moved to the couch and tentatively put out a hand. Talon's skin was cold. So was the other man's.

He stared at them.

The looks on their faces were so serene and peaceful.

Jeff broke his stare and drew his hand back.

But as peaceful as they looked, he knew they were both dead.

Epilogue

Cara drank her coffee and tried to keep from staring at the stunning blond woman two tables over from her. She'd never seen her in here before. *Was she new in town?*

The woman glanced up at her.

Their eyes locked.

Oh shit. She caught me staring.

The woman smiled, as if she'd known Cara had been looking at her.

Cara awkwardly smiled back.

The woman slid her chair back and got up from the table.

She walked toward Cara.

Shit. Now I've done it. Cara wanted to hide.

"I'm Julianna." The woman proffered a hand to Cara.

"I'm Cara Davidson," she said, trying for some decorum.

"I'm new here in town. I work just down the block at Parker and Sloan." Julianna smiled warmly.

"Oh, advertising. I'm right across the street," Cara said, silently pleased the woman worked so close by.

"The Times?"

"Yes, I'm a journalist. Human interest. With a twist." Cara gave the quirk of a grin.

"Intriguing." Julianna cocked her head to the side. "I'll have to read you work. I would love to chat more, but I don't want to be late. It's only my second week." Julianna fluffed and tossed her hair, saying, "Do you come here often?"

"Every day. Well, work days, anyway. Sometimes non-work days too. I love their coffee."

"Yes, it is very good. Here, you get my first one." Julianna reached into her purse and handed Cara a card. "I just got them."

Cara glanced at the business card. "Julianna Declan— Attorney at Law."

"Gotta run. Call me. Maybe we can do dinner some night this week." Julianna gave a little wave and went out the door.

Cara wanted to run after her and say, "How about tonight?" She needed not to be too anxious. Maybe tomorrow?

Cara grabbed her things and threw down a couple of dollars. She walked out the door and looked to the right, hoping to spot Julianna.

There she was, maybe two hundred feet away, glancing down. *Possibly texting.*

Cara followed the beautiful blond woman down the sidewalk. They'd only spoken for a couple of minutes in the coffee shop, but there'd been a connection. Julianna had approached *her*, after all. And she did say, "Call me."

Cara was intrigued and excited.

She followed closely behind Julianna, trying not to be conspicuous, but also trying to keep pace. This was the direction she also needed to be going in as well.

Julianna, however, was paying no attention. She was still looking down, absorbed. But it gave Cara the opportunity to admire her from the back. *Very nice.*

Julianna stopped at the corner for the light.

Cara was now within a few feet of her. She wanted to say something to her, maybe ask about dinner the following night. She reached up to tap Julianna on the shoulder.

Julianna stepped off the curb... and into an oncoming cab.

Cara screamed and threw herself at the woman.

They both fell to the ground—the cab missing them by inches.

Cara was on top of the woman, staring down at her.

"Oh my God, are you all right?" Cara said, trying to get up.

"Yes, I'm fine. Thank you." Julianna got up and began brushing herself off.

Cara also tried to put herself back together, adjusting the sleeves and collar on her blouse. "That was close. Are you sure you're all right?" She looked into the woman's eyes.

Recognition.

Julianna stared at her and said, "I knew you'd come back for me... Martin."

Cara automatically responded, "Of course, I did, Johnny. I promised I would."

GEMINI

Gemini—The Twins

Traits: Adaptable, Versatile, Witty, Communicative, Youthful, Lively, Loves novelty and the unusual, enjoys variety in life, Dislikes being alone.

Taylor was at shortstop; I was at second. The bases were loaded with nobody out—the final game of the State championship. We were one run up in the bottom of the ninth. Our pitcher began his wind-up. Taylor glanced at me and winked. Our signal. He took a step to his left as the pitcher released the ball. I moved to my right toward the base.

Crack!

The batter sent a line drive up the middle. Taylor leaped into the air. *Yes!* He caught it, fell to the ground, rolled, and flipped the ball to me all in one smooth set of motions. Already on the base, I caught the ball and fired it to the first baseman. He caught it and... *yes!* A triple play! Both runners had been caught off base, never expecting Taylor to make such an incredible catch.

But I knew; I always knew. That's what made us such a great combination, the sixth sense in communication between us.

And now we were the State champs, the perfect end to our senior year. We were both seventeen and all was right with the world. But I had no idea that more would come.

We celebrated our victory that night with our first kiss.

A hot kiss.

Really hot.

Maybe, with all the excitement of the game, or the beer, or maybe, the right time had come.

We'd gone out with the team after the game, not even bothering to shower or change. We'd wanted everyone to know who we were. The State champs!

After we'd all way overdone it on pizza and Cokes, one of the guys, Brat Feeney, (His real name was Brett, but he was this little, weasely guy and sometimes he could really get on your nerves, like a little bratty brother. So... Brat.) invited us over to his house for some *real* celebrating. His parents were gone for the weekend and he'd already ordered a keg, knowing we'd win. Even if we'd lost, he'd figured we'd need something to drown our sorrows.

We drank and partied for hours. All our folks knew we'd be celebrating, so it was cool. We'd earned it. Taylor kept my glass full, (Not because he was trying to get me drunk. He did this at all the parties. He wanted me to have fun.) so I had no idea how many beers I'd downed, let alone the ones we'd chugged every time someone yelled, "We're number one!" I do remember being in the bathroom a couple of times and making myself throw up. Taylor told me it was a good idea, so that we didn't get too drunk, then we could drink more. It made sense at the time. And we were drunk, and everyone else was doing it too. But the second time I went in to purge myself, the bathroom smelled really nasty. A couple of guys had missed the bowl. Of course, the smell alone made it much easier to empty my gut. Man, I did not want to be Brat tomorrow when he had to clean this place up. He was gonna *need* the whole weekend.

Then, shortly after my second hurling, things got kind of fuzzy, and the next thing I knew Taylor said it was time to go. I tried to argue, but he said we needed to go before we got stuck cleaning things up. I thought about the "vomit room" and quickly agreed.

Taylor drove home. I lived close to Brat. Taylor said he was fine to drive the few blocks through the neighborhood and that he'd sobered up a lot while I'd been heaving. I must have fallen asleep in the car, because the next thing I knew, we'd wound up in my bedroom.

Taylor said, "Be quiet."

I guess I was too loud, so I tried to whisper, "It's okay. Mom's asleep by now." Not that I knew what "by now" was. We were lying on my bed reminiscing about the game and congratulating ourselves on being the first two co-MVPs ever. I had my head resting on Taylor's stomach (which was hard and rippled, but I liked having my head there anyway, and he didn't mind) and stared up at ceiling, fascinated by the meringue-like peaks in the stucco.

Taylor brushed a hand through my hair. "After all, how could they choose between us for MVP... even if I am better looking."

"Yeah, you are," I said.

I guess it was out loud because he leaned up over me, gave me a huge grin, and punched my chest. "Move." He pushed me off him.

He got up off the bed, stripped of his shirt, and smelled it. "Whew! It kinda smells like the locker room in here. Maybe you should take your shirt off too."

I obliged, with a little help from Taylor as I couldn't seem to find the way out after I covered my face. I sat there on the edge of the bed, staring at him. He had a great body, lean, yet well-muscled and smooth. His long, curly blond hair and hazel eyes suited him perfectly.

"There, that's better," he said. He watched me watch him, his gaze intent. "Come here. Give me a hug, my man."

I stood and stepped into his open arms.

He held me firmly to him... for quite a while. Then, "You *are* the best, you know," he whispered in my ear and pressed his naked torso against mine. "You've got great looks, a killer body, and you're the best *damn* second baseman I've ever seen." He rubbed my back and arms, and I drank in the heady scent of him. I think I'd gotten that word from one of Mom's romance novels. Heady. His smell, sweaty and musky, went to my head. Both of them. I'm sure he could tell, too. We were practically glued together: chest to chest, crotch to crotch. He wasn't soft either. But he didn't let me go. It was incredible.

"You too," I mumbled.

"Huh?"

"You too. Good looking... and second base... and all."

He pulled back slightly from me, our faces only inches apart. "You're still drunk. Shortstop, I play shortstop. But you got the good-looking part right." He laughed lightly. His hot—and minty?— breath blew across my face. (He must have brushed his teeth. I hoped I had too. Ugh. *Vomit Breath*.) "I made you use mouthwash," he said. (Mind reader.)

"Oh. Thanks. And I know you play short. I just meant... Do you really think I'm good-looking?"

He laughed again and moved even closer, his lips but a minty-breath away. "Are you kidding? With that cute, spiky blond hair..." He ruffled it. "Those great pecs and abs..." He rubbed *his* great pecs and abs against mine. "And those deep hazel eyes..." He peered into mine.

And that's when it happened.

His lips touched mine, slowly, tentatively, then—ever so slightly—more aggressively.

I didn't think. I couldn't. I just felt. His lips were so soft, like velvet and butter. And intoxicating. Much more so than the countless beers I'd had earlier.

I'm not sure how long the kiss lasted, but I didn't want it to stop.

It did. Taylor slowly withdrew his lips from mine, but stayed within my breath. "I love you, you know. I always have, since we were little."

Did he mean, like a brother? We'd always been close, pretty much inseparable.

"Not like a brother, Tommy."

I *know* I'd hadn't spoken aloud *that* time. He'd read my thoughts. Again. "Me too. I guess."

He pulled back and punched me in the chest. Hard. *"I guess? You asshole!"*

He threw me down on the bed and fell on top of me. This time he kissed me long and hard, branding me. When he stopped, he leaned into my face with his arms propped on either side of me, holding himself up. "I guess?" He wiggled his hips against mine. "It certainly feels like more than, 'I guess?'"

"I know. I meant, I know." I needed him on me again. I pulled him back down to me. His hands were everywhere, stroking, caressing, squeezing. Mine followed suit.

"These have to go," he said. He snapped open my baseball pants and pushed them down my legs, the stretchy, tight nylon frustrating him—and me—as he struggled to get them off me. He stood and looked down at me. "God, you look so hot in just your jock." I felt myself blush and put my hands over my crotch, trying to hide my obvious erection. "Don't. Let me look. I've thought about this for a long time. Every time I see you in the locker room just wearing that, I think of this scene right now. Why do you think I always have to go to the bathroom before I change too?"

"Weak bladder?"

He grinned. He put his hands to his stretchy waistband and pulled it away from his body. He looked down inside at himself. "Nope. This is why. You wanna see me too?

I nodded, my mouth dry.

His eyes burned into mine as he slowly slid the tight pants down his legs. "Well?"

I couldn't breathe, let alone talk.

"You want the whole banana." He grinned again at the obvious pun, his fingers now just inside the waistband of his jock.

I found my voice. "More than anything I've ever wanted." And meant it.

"This is going to be the best night of our lives. This was meant to be, Tommy. Our lives together so far have all been leading up to this moment. I've never felt this way about anyone... nor wanted anyone more. I wanted you to know this up front. After this, there's no turning back. You get that, right?"

"Right," I said, meaning it, and getting it. I knew in that moment that this *was* meant to be. He was my destiny. He was why I never really looked at anyone else. I only wanted him. "I only want you, Taylor."

I'm all yours." He revealed himself fully to me. "Forever."

* * *

I slept peacefully that night, curled in his arms. Next morning, when I woke to the sounds of Mom knocking, Taylor was gone.

When I finally saw him later that day, he acted as if nothing had changed between us—but everything had. Or maybe it hadn't. Maybe all the feelings we had now for each other had always been there, lying dormant. Now, they were out in the open, at least for us. We didn't have to hide anything from one another. It was a great feeling.

The rest of the weekend was like a dream. Taylor would spend the night in my bed, and then be gone when I awoke.

Monday, however, brought us a new set of problems. "Tommy, did you see the newspaper?" Taylor yelled down the school hallway that morning. "They called us 'Baseball's Golden Boys,' I guess 'cuz of our blond hair and *golden gloves!*" he screamed.

"And the school paper's calling you 'The Dynamite Duo,', T 'n' T, Taylor and Tommy." This announcement came from our first baseman, Greg Evans, who was standing with me at my locker.

Greg was tall and lean, which helped him a lot at first base. He had a pleasant face with wavy brown locks, which were just a hair too long, and he kept brushing off his forehead. Coach was always on him to get it cut. "Cuz one of these days," he'd say, "it's gonna get in your eyes and you won't see the ball comin' and... POW! Right in the schnazola. Taylor and I both liked him a lot. "I hear two different farm clubs have made offers to you guys. Who are you gonna to go with?"

"I don't know," Taylor said. "Did you hear that Tommy? Dyn-o-mite!"

He punched me in the arm.

"You guys are Dyn-o-mite." Greg again. "It's like you guys read each other's minds or something. I mean, Taylor you *always* know where the batter is gonna hit, and Tommy, you're always at the base miles before the runner. And with your guys' arms... they're the fastest double plays I've ever seen! And that *triple* play... I thought my freakin' arm was gonna come outta the socket from that throw, Tommy!"

"Yeah, we're dynamite together," I said, laughing. "Yep, dynamite on and off the field."

Taylor punched me in the gut. "Oof!"

"You guys really are. I'm so glad you're my friends." Greg quieted. "I'm gonna miss you guys come the fall."

"Hey, we'll keep in touch. After all, you are a part of the 'Dyn-o-mite' triple play! Our third of the season—another record, I might add." I put my arm around his shoulder and hugged him to me.

"Thanks," Greg said shyly. "You know, you Golden Boys are gonna have your pick of the girls for Senior Prom. Not that you didn't before. Man, I wish I had half your guys' looks."

"Hey, Greg, you can hold your own. There's Brittany Wells and Lisa Pettibone. They've got the hots for you," I said.

"Yeah, maybe. But I think they just like me 'cuz I hang with you guys."

"You're probably right," Taylor said very seriously, then laughed. "Guess you'll just to have hang with us for the rest of your *life.*" We all laughed. Taylor continued, "Or at least until your dick falls off from all the girls we score for you!"

"So who *are* you guys gonna take?"

"I don't know," Taylor said. "We don't want to make anyone mad or jealous... maybe we'll take each other." I shot an anxious glance at Taylor.

Greg laughed again. "Well, you guys'd be the best looking couple there!"

"Ain't it the truth. Ain't it the truth." Taylor did his best Cowardly Lion impression. As we all laughed some more, a fantasy played out in my mind: Who would be king, and who would be queen? Two kings, I decided.

* * *

Prom! Ugh! What were we going to do? Who would we take? Wait. Why was I worrying? We could just double-date like we always did. Sure. We could go to the prom, go to a party, lose the girls, get a hotel room. And Taylor and I could party all night. It was Prom after all. It was expected that we would stay out all night.

That's just what we did.

And it *was* a Prom night to remember.

As for pro ball, that would have to wait a while. Mom was very happy that Taylor and I had been made the farm club offers. "But," she told me, "you need a college education. Your father would have wanted that. Baseball won't last forever."

We argued a little, but my heart wasn't in it. Mom had had it hard since Dad died three years ago, and she didn't need any more grief. I couldn't bear to see her disappointed. Taylor agreed with me. And we could train more and get just that much better at baseball so we could have our pick of who we wanted to play for. I really didn't care who we played for, as long as I had Taylor by my side—on and off the field.

So, off I went to college with Taylor in tow. He agreed that an education wouldn't hurt us, and as he said on our long drive to college, "We're still gonna play ball while we're there. We've got full scholarships. But mostly, we'll be together. We always will be, Tommy. I hope you know that. I'm yours; you're mine. No matter what happens in our lives or our careers, I'll be there. You're my life..."

I couldn't respond. He looked so lovingly into my eyes, which were filled with tears, and smiled. "Forever."

That magic word: forever. Life was great.

* * *

College life was terrific. We shared a dorm room. (How convenient.) We made a lot of friends (thanks to Taylor), partied, played a lot of ball, and made a lot of love (also thanks to Taylor). Actually, I had a lot to do with that too. After that first night with him back in high school, I became some kind of animal. I wanted sex all the time. Fortunately, so did he. He never turned me down—or even hesitated. He was always up for me (literally) and rarin' to go. I must have secreted some kind of vibe or pheromone scent, or maybe it was our "freaky" sixth sense with one another, but he always knew when I wanted it.

We never really had any steady girlfriends. We would double-date, occasionally, to keep up a good front. But for some reason girls wouldn't push us for any kind of lasting relationship or even a second date. It was like they just wanted to be with us and have a good time, not *date* us. (Let alone the other things. Ugh.) They knew Taylor and I were best friends, a team, and that it somehow wouldn't be right to split us up. No one ever said, or even hinted at the fact, that we might be gay or (gasp) lovers, which was perfect for us, and we never let anyone know any differently. Life couldn't get any better. Could it? Yes, it could.

* * *

One night at the end of our sophomore year, Taylor and I were lying in bed, exhausted after our championship win, as well as our championship lovemaking, and I said, "Now that I've won Mom over and she's realized that we can actually have real careers in baseball—I actually think it was that offer from the Dodgers that did the trick, you know she's always hated them. Anyway, so just as long as we play for anyone *but* the Dodgers, she's all for it."

Taylor nodded to humor my rambling as he slowly painted a streak up my leg with his tongue. (He was insatiable. Just like me.) When he finally struck gold, I grasped his head in my hands and raised it.

"Something wrong?" He was all wide-eyed innocence. "Doesn't look like it." His eyes glanced down at my obvious interest.

"I was asking you a question."

"Really? I don't remember hearing your voice go up at end of a sentence. Of course, something went up, I see." His grin would have made me weak-kneed except that I was lying down.

"I just have one question and then you may continue what you were doing."

"And that is?" His tongue lashed out.

I gasped. "Please..."

"Your wish is my command." He opened his mouth wide.

Once again I grabbed his head. Reluctantly. "Since we've decided to join the Big Leagues next season, who do you want to play for?"

"I leave all the decisions to you." He grabbed my hand and held it. "Money, careers, friends, how many times we make love..." He lapped the inside of my hand and turned onto his side, gazing up at me, his eyes dark and intense.

"You know you're the one who makes all the friends," I said, reaching down and giving his nipple a playful pinch, which I knew he loved. "Everybody loves you. You're always smiling—"

"Because of you." He moved down my body and bowed his head again. He stuck out his tongue and licked me.

I tried to ignore it. My body's lurching kind of belied that. "You're always happy—"

"Because of you." Another lick.

"You never get angry or upset—"

A very long slow lick. "Because of you." He slid up my torso and pulled me into his arms for a truly amazing kiss. I guess the constant nipple play had gotten to him.

When I recovered from the kiss, I said, "Well, I guess, maybe we do complement one another."

"In *every* way." He leered. And slid back down my body to show me.

* * *

The big leagues sure were: the pay, the publicity, the pressure... all of it. But it was great. With Taylor at my side, on and off the field, we conquered it all. We played better than we ever had in our lives. Our psychic connection was stronger than ever. Fans, reporters, and even our teammates were all amazed at our incredible, intuitive connection. Actually, it had been growing stronger since the first night Taylor and I had been *together*. We were in all the magazines (*Sports Illustrated* covers twice in one year) and newspapers. We did a few television shows. We even guest starred as ourselves on a short lived sit-com. (Although, that episode gave them their highest ratings.) We had to act like we were both in love with the lead actress on the show to make her boyfriend jealous. I'm pretty sure the actor playing the boyfriend was gay too. So in all actuality, none of us guys would have been interested in her in real life. (Ah, the illusion of television.)

The Golden Boys! It was always in the headlines. The fans would chant it in the stadiums. They'd hold up banners. Sometimes the fans would revive the "T 'n' T" chant too. We'd spend hours signing autographs for fans. Taylor loved it. And I have to admit, I did too. He loved to see the smiles on people's faces. And he made sure he never signed an autograph alone. I always had to sign with him, and I made sure he did the same for me. It was odd that no one ever questioned why we did that. I guess fans were more than happy to get both of the "T 'n' T" signatures. Sometimes, if a fan would walk away before we both had signed, Taylor would go after him and jokingly say to the fan, "You can't have just one Golden Boy, you've gotta have us both. I couldn't play without the other half of the *best* double play in baseball!" he would shout and laugh, and everyone would cheer.

Another curious phenomenon was the lack of questions we received about our personal lives. Reporters would ask us about girls and dates, but you could tell they weren't really interested. The tabloids would occasionally link one of us with some girl or other (as they did with all celebrities—especially single ones), but no one paid any attention to that either. We would tell stories of our high school and college lives and everyone would be rapt as Taylor would dramatize some past game and give it all the drama and suspense of the best M. Night Shyamalan thriller. It was crazy really. All anyone cared about was the two of us. Together. As if no one wanted to see anyone come between us. We were special; we were America's heroes. We were "The Golden Boys." Untouchable.

* * *

And for the next six years it went that way. We were in every All-Star game. (You couldn't split up the best double play combination in baseball.) We each won two Golden Glove awards (How appropriate.) in those same years. Our team was first in our division every year. And we won two World Series. In the first one Taylor and I were named co-MVPs. The first time in World Series history! What could be better?

"What could be better?" I asked Taylor as we lay in bed after some seriously mind-blowing, as well as other things, lovemaking, on the night of our last game of our sixth season. We'd won our division, but lost to St. Louis in the final game of the playoffs.

"Better? You, me, a desert island in the South Pacific."

"Anytime," I joked and nuzzled into his armpit.

"Tomorrow. 10:00 A. M."

I put my face to his. "You're kidding. Right?"

"Nope. Reach under your pillow."

I pulled out the envelope with the tickets. I read them closely. I bolted up from the bed. "Taylor. We need to pack. Now!"

"Already done. Besides, heh, heh, we're not going to be wearing very much."

I looked at him, as he ran a hand down that perfect naked body of his. "You're the greatest," I choked out. The tears started. He was always catching me off guard like this. How could there be anyone better than he was? I was convinced there was no love greater than ours.

"There is no love greater than ours," he said simply. "Come here." I knelt on the bed beside him. He rubbed his thumb beneath my eye, brushing away the tears. "And if we like this tropical paradise, we can make an offer on the island—as our place to retire to." He licked his thumb.

"Yes," I said and sniffed. "That'll be perfect. Just the two of us. After all, we can't play ball forever—at least baseball." I smirked and sniffed again. "And I *do* think that sooner or later people are going to figure out some things about us."

"Yep. It's inevitable. But we've been lucky up till now, for whatever reason. That's why I decided on our very own private island. If things get too crazy, we have a place to go for the rest of our lives. Sun. Sand. And—"

"Sex."

He arched an eyebrow. "No. *You,*" he said, tweaking my nose. "You're ESP is on the fritz."

I felt myself blush. Of course it was me. I knew that. But sometimes I just have to make myself believe that it's all real. That Taylor is real. And that he loves me above all and always will.

* * *

Before we left the next day, I told Taylor we had to stop and see Mom, and say goodbye.

She was waiting for us in the living room. The bright yellow sun dress belied the concern on her face.

"What's wrong? I asked.

Her hands were clasped in her lap. I remembered the last time she looked like this. It was to say that Dad was dead. I pulled Taylor down onto the couch facing her.

"I have to tell you boys something I should have told you a long time ago, before things went too far, but I promised your father I wouldn't. Now, I fear I made the wrong decision."

My stomach clenched in a knot.

"When I got pregnant, we were just eking by, but instead of having an abortion... Even now it's hard for me to say that word. Your father and I decided that somehow we would make it work. But, as fate would have it, I gave birth to not one, but *two* beautiful little boys. We had no idea what we were going to do. Finally, we made the decision to let my Aunt Betty raise one of them. She had always wanted a child but couldn't have one. Her husband had died and she was alone. She wasn't ready to remarry, even though she was only thirty. Some people just feel that there is only one person for them. I certainly felt that way. But that's neither here nor there. We felt that a baby might help give her life some purpose, and we knew the child would be well cared for and we would know where he was. Two years later she got very ill. We went to see her and she asked us if we would take her little boy and raise him. We were doing much better by then. Your father had gotten a promotion and we could now afford to raise another child. We had always regretted our choice and now we had the opportunity to rectify it. So, now we had our son back, but we'd decided to tell him and others that he was adopted. We just couldn't explain to him why we didn't want him in the first place, or why we chose one over the other. We didn't. We tossed a coin. A *coin*," she wailed and buried her face in her hands. "I'm so sorry, Taylor."

It had been Taylor. But did it matter? I had remained silent throughout. Taylor rushed to Mom and hugged her.

The ramifications of this insane revelation were only beginning to form in my thoughts.

"It's all right, Mom. You *could* have told me. I *do* understand," Taylor said.

I'm glad one of us does. I don't understand. I don't understand anything. We looked a lot alike, but I thought that was coincidence, you know, the way we dressed similarly and had our hair cut. I mean, we did grow up together. We were obviously not identical twins. But pretty close. It kind of explained the psychic connection. I'd always heard twins had a special relationship. But not *this* special.

"I love you both so much, and I want you to be happy. I know you love each other very much. I always want you to take care of one another. It's just..." She broke down again.

"It's okay, Mom. Tommy and I have it all worked out. (We do?) Everything will be fine."

"I believe you, Taylor. You always did know how to make things right." She turned to me. "Tommy, are you all right? You know your brother loves you very much. (Oh, I know it. And you don't want to.) He's always taken care of you. He is the older one, by the way." She half-smiled. "Please, Tommy, say something. You're making me worry."

Automatically, it came out, "Don't worry, Mom. I'm fine. (Lie.) It's just a bit of a surprise. (Like the D-Day Invasion) Things'll work out. It'll be an adjustment. (Starting with no more mind-blowing, earth-shattering, tear-the-room-apart sex.)

"I don't want you two to adjust or change anything. You keep going on as you are—loving each other. If anything, you should feel even closer." (If anything) She looked directly into my eyes for several seconds. *She's reading my mind. She knows everything. Moms know everything.* My mind froze.

She smiled at both of us and stood up. "Now, you boys get going or you'll miss your incredible trip."

I gave a sudden puzzled look to her then back at Taylor. He looked sheepish.

"Taylor called me last week and told me all about it," she said. "It sounds wonderful." She hugged me and said, "No matter what, I'll always hold both of you deep in my heart. No one could ever be more precious or special to me than you both are. You've both done so much and will *do* so much. Together. Always. Forever." Big tears were ready to pour down her cheeks.

I hugged her and mumbled a "Thanks" and "I love you, Mom."

✳ ✳ ✳

73

"What have we done?" I blurted to Taylor as we drove away from the house. "And does she know? It sure sounded like it."

"Tommy, calm down. I think maybe she does, but she's okay with it. She knows how much we love each other."

"But Taylor, what happens when everyone else finds out? Taylor! It's a crime! We can't love each other. Let alone f—"

"*Tommy.* Calm down. No one needs to know. Mom will destroy the records."

"But the hospital has records!"

"Why would anyone check?"

"Because when they find out we're gay, they'll check out *everything.*"

"How will they find out we're gay?"

"I don't know. They just will. They always do." I was blathering.

"I'm not going to tell them. And if you don't, then nobody will know. It's not like there are a bunch of other guys I've slept with who could tell. And you haven't slept with anybody else." He paused. "Have you? I mean, I never asked you. I never thought about it. But I guess you could've." His voice had genuine angst in it. How could he think I would ever cheat on him? With who? There were guys that probably would've slept with me, but why would I? Taylor's the hottest guy I've ever seen. *I'm* the one should be asking this question.

"You really never thought about it?" We were stopped at a light.

He looked at me. "No. You've always been the only one I was interested in." His eyes misted up.

"Pull up over there in that gas station and park. You can't drive if you can't see."

Taylor made a quick left through the light and parked. Now the tears were flowing. I needed to relieve his agony. This wasn't right. *At least I can fix this.*

"Taylor, stop crying. You never cry."

"I can't help it. I thought that... *sniff*... I was the only... *sniff*..." He rubbed the snot from his nose with his hand. "That you and I... *sniff*..."

"Taylor, you *are* the only one. How could you ever think I would sleep with anyone else? And no, I've never thought about it either, that you might've slept with another guy until now. It's us. Only us. We're it. Okay? Done? You going to stop crying now—little baby?"

"*Ow.*" Taylor punched me in the chest.

"Don't be an asshole. I love you, you jerk. And if I wanna cry over you, I will. Got it?"

He slugged me again. "*Ow.* Stop it. That hurts."

"Who's the baby now?" He sniffed once more and rubbed away some more snot. Then he grinned. "You really don't want any other guys? Only me?"

"How many times do I have to tell you?"

"For the rest of our lives." He grabbed my hand and kissed it. *God, I love him.*

75

"Here's what we're going to do. We'll quit baseball. Right now. We've got more money than we could ever need. We'll buy our island, live there, and everyone will eventually forget all about us. We'll be yesterday's news in no time. You know how fickle the press and the public are."

Taylor. Always pragmatic.

"Tommy? Do you love me?"

"You know I do."

"Then that's it. We love each other, and screw the rest of the world if they can't handle it. It's our lives, not *theirs*. Nobody should be able to tell us *how* to live or *who* to love. We love each other; that will never change. So if *they* won't change the rules, we'll make up our own. It's only society that says two siblings can't love one another, and you know they meant a man and a woman. That's because of the whole getting pregnant and having a twisted kid thing. But we don't have to worry about that. I'm not pregnant. Are you?" (How could he joke right now?) "So we're good. Look at European royalty. They married their brothers or sisters all the time and no one said a thing. I can't just turn off a switch and say I don't love you anymore. My heart doesn't work like that. When you know deep down that something is right, you go with it. And *we're* right. (Whew. He could sell lottery tickets to Death Row inmates.) Taylor waited for my response.

I was silent. Then, eventually, I said, "It's hard for a second baseman to make a double play without his shortstop." I gave him a sly little grin.

"All right. South Pacific, here we come!" Taylor bellowed.

We got on the plane bound for... I can't even remember the funky little name of the island, but Taylor said after we landed we needed to take a small boat to get there.

However...

The plane never made it. All onboard disappeared somewhere in the South Pacific. The bodies were never recovered. And Taylor and I never got to see our island paradise.

* * *

But Taylor and I did find our Paradise together. And, believe me, it's a lot better than some desert island.

Taylor holds my hand and we look down on Mom. She's remarried now. He is a wonderful husband to her, Harry (of all the awful names), and she seems happy. Taylor and I kind of pushed her into it. Even though she had said there was one great love of your life, (I was, and always would be, with mine right now.) you could find another kind of happiness with someone else.

She shouldn't be alone. She'd been through and done so much. Things only a mother could do. She is in the living room, staring up at the blown-up poster over the fireplace. She always knows when we're looking in on her. (A cool perk of being in the hereafter.) I'd given her the poster after we'd won our first World Series. It read: THE GOLDEN BOYS OF BASEBALL in huge block letters, and in smaller lettering, "Double MVPs—Double plays." (We'd won the final game with one of our famous double plays.)

She always smiled broadly at that phrase: The Golden Boys. She loved the play on words with our last name. Golden. Taylor and Tommy Golden. Mom's twin Golden Boys.

CANCER

Cancer-The Crab

Traits: Emotional, Loving, Intuitive, Imaginative, Cautious, Protective, Sympathetic, Overemotional, Touchy, Unable to let go.

Present

Seamus

My name is Father Seamus Mulligan... yes, I'm Irish. I'm fifty-two years old. And in my thirty years as a priest, this is the first time I'm doubting my vows, and I don't know what to do. Two hours ago, my protégé and friend, Father Kell Vidnovic confessed to me feelings for one of our parishioners—a male parishioner. Then, to ice the proverbial cake, this parishioner, an hour later, came into my confessional and professed *his* desire for *my* priest.

Dear Lord—Help Me.

Present

Kell

My name is Kell Vidnovic. I'm half-Irish, half-Serbian. It's different, I know. I turned thirty-one a month ago. I just confessed to my mentor and friend, Father Seamus, that I'm falling for one of our parishioners. Seamus and I had never discussed my sexuality. Now he knows. I dread disappointing him. After all he's done for me, the guidance and support, I couldn't bear to lose him. For the first time I'm doubting my vows—my calling.

Heavenly Father, I need your help.

Present

Race

My name is Race Corcorran. I'm Irish and German. I was a model in New York. Now I'm trying to start a new life here in Pittsburgh. I like it here. I like my church and I love my priest. No, I *really* love my priest. Father Kell Vidnovic. I know it's wrong, and impossible. However, I think he has feelings for me, too. But he's a priest. He took a vow of celibacy, which is one thing I'll never understand. I wouldn't have survived a week in the priesthood. I like sex too much.

Now I've gone and confessed my feelings to Father Seamus, maybe a mistake, but I've always been impetuous. Why would God do this to me? It's so unfair. Maybe karma for my, uh, transgressions. I'm trying to be good now. I go to church all the time... and not just to see Kell, but for guidance.

God, if ever I needed your guidance, it's now.

Two hours Ago

Seamus

"Father Seamus, I need you to hear my confession," Kell said to me. "I should have told you a couple of weeks ago, but I didn't think things would get so out of control."

I stared into Kell's tear-filled eyes. "Kell, what is it? You can tell me anything. We've been friends and fellow priests for over ten years now."

"I know, Seamus. I even spent my twenty-first birthday with you, instead of in Las Vegas." He half-smiled. "I have no one else to turn to. I'm so frustrated and confused... and afraid. Afraid to tell you most of all. I don't want you to hate me or be disappointed in me. I couldn't take it. You mean so much to me." He began to cry in earnest now.

I moved closer to him on my office sofa and put my arm around his shoulders. I'd always heard his confession in my office. That's the kind of relationship we had. And right now, I was very glad of it. My Kell was hurting. I hadn't seen such pain in his eyes since his parents and younger sister had been killed in a car accident by a drunk driver, which happened in his first year here at the parish. He was devastated, of course, but he survived and prayed fervently, ultimately accepting God's will. His faith has always been unwavering. But now, with that look on his face... this was something totally different. Kell was in trouble, and he'd come to me for help.

"Kell, my boy, please, tell me. We can get through this, whatever it may be. Trust me."

He shook his head violently and cried harder.

My heart broke for him. He was such a good boy—man, really. He was thirty-one, kind, gentle, and good-looking. With his blond hair and build, I told him he could have been the next Robert Redford; they looked so much alike. But the Holy Father had other designs for him.

His sobbing began to subside as he clung closer to me.

"Seamus," he choked. "I... I think I'm in love."

I stopped patting his shoulder. Love? Had one of our fair lady parishioners captured his heart? Which woman could have been so selfish, and foolish? "I'm going to get you a nice snifter of brandy to help settle you down. Then you can start at the beginning and tell me the whole thing. I'm here for you, Kell, and God willing, I always will be."

"I hope so." He snuffled.

After I let him drink a good bit of my favorite brandy, I tried again. "Now take your time and start from the first. It is one of our parishioners, I assume?"

He nodded.

"How did you meet?"

"After Sunday service, the eleven o'clock, about a month ago. We started talking about the area. The city. He'd just recently moved here..."

"He?" Did I hear right?

"Yes. You mean you didn't know I'm..."

"No. I never actually thought about it." It was true I hadn't. "It didn't... doesn't matter. We're priests."

"This isn't an epiphany for me, Seamus. I've always known. In high school there were a couple of guys that I... well, you know. And I knew it wasn't just 'experimenting,' at least not for me. I was attracted to them. I had feelings for them—one in particular, but he didn't feel the same way about me."

I kept silent, as I recalled a buried memory of my own.

"When I took my vow of celibacy, I was fine with it. There was no one special and my devotion was strong. I knew this was where I belonged." He began to tear up again. "And all these years there has been no one to even tempt me. Until now... Why?" I saw anger flare in his eyes. "Why would God do this to me?"

This was not the Kell I knew at all. He never got angry.

"And don't give me those platitudes about 'God is testing you,' or 'He works in mysterious ways.' They're words used an excuse when a priest has nothing useful to say. And you know it."

I could only nod. They were overused phrases, as true as they may be. They weren't blarney, just overused. And then, I don't know how it slipped out of my stupid mouth, I said, "We'll pray on it." He stared at me with a look I instantly wanted to forget. "Och, Kell, forgive me. What an imbecilic thing to say. I *have* nothing to say and it just came out."

His eyes softened. "Seamus, it's all right." He half-smiled. "You proved my point. I don't blame you. I probably would have said something equally banal. It comes with the territory. And, actually, I have been praying about it. Hard. I *do* believe the Holy Father will help guide me. I wish He'd hurry up, though." He looked pleadingly into my eyes. "You'll help me... work it out?"

Thank God he wasn't mad at me. "Of course *we'll* work it out. There are always solutions. Sometimes difficult ones. I don't want you to despair. I am—and always will be—here for you. You're my own. My family." I put my hand on his knee to reassure him. He clutched it tightly with his own.

"Thank you. Thank you, Seamus. I love you."

"I love you, too, dear boy. And don't ever doubt it. Why don't you stay here for a while and relax. I have some confessions to hear." I needed time to process all this. "We'll talk some more later."

He nodded.

Kell

Seamus closed his office door. I stared into space. My eyes were dry now. I thought I would feel better telling him. I was hoping he would have a solution. I was hoping for a miracle. I still am. I know I'm being naïve. I *am* naïve—at least about love. Thank you, God, for letting Seamus understand. Now, please help *me* understand. Is Race some kind of test?

Race. Tall, trim, fit, ridiculously handsome with his black wavy hair, misty-blue eyes, square jaw, iconic features, and that gorgeous, ready smile... I sound like some teenage girl. I can't help my feelings. But he's also kind, funny, charming—and lost. Why did I think I could help him? I should have avoided meeting him. I should have ignored the attraction. And I *never* should have said "yes" to coffee with him.

Two Weeks Ago

"How do you like your coffee?" Race's perfect smile followed the question.

"Black," I said.

"Me too." He smiled.

Trouble. His wink made my stomach flutter... and a little bit further down. I thought those feelings were dormant, or even dead. I felt the heat rush up through my body and into my face.

"Now, that's adorable. You blush. Are priests allowed to do that?" He flashed that electric smile again. He should be a model.

"So, Race, I know you're new to Pittsburgh. What do you do?" I had to say something and not just stare at him.

"I've been here two months now. I was modeling in New York."

I gave a short intake of breath. "Anything I might have seen?"

"Possibly, but I kind of hope not. I modeled mostly underwear. There was this national ad campaign, a year ago, that I did for these mesh-style briefs. There were billboards everywhere. I thought it was just another shoot. The money was good. I had no idea it would go viral."

My thoughts raced. I thought he looked familiar. There was an enormous billboard across the freeway a few miles from here. And several months ago, it had caused quite a stir in the city. It had been quite revealing, and there had been a petition to have it taken down. The company had fought hard to keep it up, and it had remained. My face must have betrayed my recognition.

"Oh shit. You saw it. My brother said he'd seen it here. That campaign is really what made me leave New York. I was swarmed. It was great to be wanted as a model, but the blatant sexual stuff got crazy. I was already getting turned off to the business anyway. I mean, as soon as you get your clothes off in front of these guys—the asshole photographers, lighting guys... they think you're easy and ready to drop your pants and spread your legs. Oh my God, I'm sorry. That was really crude. I guess I have a little pent-up anger. Being in New York, and around those dicks kind of colored my language. Oh shit! I did it again. I'm sorry, Father. See. I do need your help." He smiled again, uncomfortably.

Still dazzling. I was guessing he was gay. But that didn't matter.

The coffee arrived. The waitress audibly sighed.

"Anything else?" a hint of hope in her voice as she moved in a little closer to Race.

"No, thank you," he said and smiled at her.

She turned away, then quickly back around. "Just let me know."

"I guess that happens often to you," I said. "And don't be worried about your language too much. We do live in a cosmopolitan city, perhaps not quite like New York, but I'm familiar with the terminology. I may not use it, but it doesn't offend me. And I'm sure your billboard sold a lot of underwear. We do live in the age where sex sells. I'm not a fool to hide from it. It's everywhere. I take it as a matter of course."

"Thanks, I knew you were cool, as well as..." He paused. "Nevermind. I've already put my foot pretty far down my throat."

"Please. I'm really unoffendable, Race. You can be frank with me."

He stared directly into my eyes, no expression on his face. "Hot. That's what I was going to say. I was going to try and be cute and say you were cool and hot at the same time." His face remained stoic. "As you can probably tell by now, I'm not used to talking to a priest—at least when I'm not in church."

I laughed. I noticed a few stares at my outburst. I couldn't help it. He was so charming and delightful, and as I'd surmised, gay. "Thank you. No one has called me 'hot' since... I can't remember. Oh, yes I do. I had the flu a couple of years ago, and when the doctor took my temperature he said, 'You're hot.'" My turn to be cute. What was I doing? I was flirting. It had been years, but that's definitely what it was. And it *did* matter that he was gay. This man was doing something to me. I was: vulnerable, disarmed, naked. I needed to leave.

"Cute," he said. "I will try to filter myself. I do know what decorum is. It's just after living in New York for a few years, I kind of forgot how to apply it. Anyway, so I've been here two months, and I kind of like it. It's not crazy like New York. I feel more human here. But I don't really know anyone besides my brother. He lives pretty close to here. So when I decided to leave New York, he let me crash with him and his wife for a few weeks. Last week, I moved into my own place, which is right around the corner. It's close to my brother and the church, and the neighborhood seems nice."

"It is," I interjected.

"I like your church. I hadn't been in years. It felt right the first time I walked into it. I'd been feeling... lost, I guess, undirected. I walked by the church, and something pulled me in."

He was staring at me again. I'd forgotten all about leaving.

"I'm not sure what I want to do. I could probably pick up some print work here, but I don't know if I want to model anymore. I kind of soured on it. I need something more permanent. It's not like I'll be good-looking forever." He dazzle-smiled me.

I doubted his statement. If anyone would be "good-looking forever," it would be him. He was perfect. Surely, God had blessed this one.

"You have an odd look on your face. You're probably thinking, 'What a conceited jerk this guy is. How do I get out of here?' I don't mean to be obnoxious about my looks. It's genetics. I didn't have anything to do with it, well, except for maybe keeping my body in shape. I have to say, a lot of times I'd just rather look ordinary. I know looks can be an asset, but sometimes they can be a burden. I have a few horror stories—and not just modeling ones. The dating scene. One word: Hell. Shit. I mean, I'm sorry. God, do you want me to leave now? You could probably be defrocked—Is that the word?—for just speaking to me."

I started to laugh. Then some more. He laughed with me.

After I dried my eyes, I said, "Have you thought about stand-up comedy as a career?"

"Ha. No, but I did think about opening a modeling school here. There doesn't seem to be a lot of competition. I've checked it out some."

"That sounds promising. I'm sure you'd be very good at it."

"Thanks for the vote of confidence. I think I'd like to try to help the up-and-comers who don't have a clue about the dog-eat-dog *real* modeling world. Give them a heads-up. Warn them. Tell them all the dos and don'ts—mostly don'ts. Maybe save some of the naifs from getting eaten alive. Explain how it can be as bad for men as it is for women. Can I make a confession to you?"

I was momentarily nonplussed. "I don't think this is quite the right place..."

"Not that kind of confession." He grinned. "Uh, Kell... Can I call you Kell? Or do I have to say 'Father?'"

"Kell is fine." I liked hearing him say my name. It rang. This was not good.

"It's a great name. Like the Book of Kells?"

"Exactly. My mother was fascinated with it ever since she was a child and saw it in Dublin at Trinity College. She loved the book's colorful illuminations. Her parents were born there."

"But not your father."

"No. His family fled Bosnia, formerly Yugoslavia, years ago and settled here in Pittsburgh."

"So you grew up here?"

"Yes."

"Where do they live now?"

"They were killed in an automobile accident with my sister several years ago."

Race covered his face and took a sip of his coffee. "I'm really sorry. My conversation skills need serious honing."

"It's all right. I can talk about it." And it was true. I felt relaxed talking to him. "I still miss them and love them, but God has his plans."

"Is that what made you become a priest?"

"No. It happened shortly after I joined the priesthood."

"You said, 'God has his plans.' Well, that's what I'm trying to figure out. Does he really?" He stared at me. I didn't think he was waiting for a response, so I kept silent. "Can I confess now?"

I nodded.

"More coffee?" The waitress filled Race's cup without his assent. "You, too?" she said, still staring at Race.

"Yes, thank you." She filled and left.

Race watched her leave, then turned to me, a serious expression now on his face. "I went to your church, one, because I needed some help and guidance, and two, because I saw *you* going into it, which I know must sound terrible. I didn't know you were a priest. I just saw this guy who looked like a young Robert Redford—which I'm sure you hear all the time—and I followed you in. You went down the aisle and out the back. I thought you worked there or something. And while I waited for you to come back out, I started looking around and—you're going to think I'm crazy—but I heard a voice say, "Yes. Here." There wasn't anyone in the church. But I knew the voice was right. I felt like I should be there. It gave me a feeling of solace and peace. I waited for a while, an hour or so, and then I left. But I knew I wanted to come back—and not just to see you—but for the feeling I got there. Now do you want to run?"

Yes, I wanted to run—run away from him. And to him. This incredibly good-looking man was attracted to me. And I to him. "I do have to get back. There is the evening service to prepare. Thank you for the coffee."

"Right. You're welcome." He looked up at the ceiling and gave a grunt of frustration. "Shit," he mumbled, then looked at me. "I was too much, wasn't I? There is that line you're not supposed to cross, and I just pole-vaulted right over it. I'm sorry, Kell... Father. Do you want me to stop coming to mass? I understand. This whole thing was stupid—"

"No. Don't stop coming to mass. I honestly enjoyed meeting you. It would bother me greatly if you stopped coming." It was true. "Have faith. Things will work out." Who was I saying this to? "And I really *do* have a service to prepare."

"Can I see you again? I mean... coffee? You've helped me out already. I am seriously going to look into the modeling school ideas thanks to your input."

"Yes, I'd like that." Had I agreed to a date? No. Coffee. That's not a date. I was helping out one of God's souls.

I was lying to myself.

Race

What am I doing? I'm falling for a *priest* for Christ's sakes. I wanted to walk him back to the church... while holding his hand, but I told him I wanted to stay and have another cup of coffee. Now, here I am surreptitiously following him back. And he looks good from the back. He'd changed into jeans and a polo shirt for our coffee date. He filled out both perfectly. He should have been the model. Great ass. I should stop my prurient thoughts, especially because it's giving me a hard-on. But I can't help it. I'm so drawn to him. He's kind, caring, funny, and genuine. I feel like I was guided to him. Divine guidance? I wish. I doubt it. A priest, really? How can this go anywhere? He's celibate. I'm so not, even if there hasn't been anyone for a while. No matter how great he is, I'd never survive without sex. Impossible. I'm not a sex maniac, but I do love it. I thought about hitting some of the bars. There's a big gay population here. But I don't want to. Not since I've seen him. Although, it would probably be better than masturbating and thinking about him, which I'm sure is a sin in itself. *Shit.* I bet I have to confess that. *Whoa. Awkward.* I'll make sure it's the older priest. Still awkward. "Bless me, Father, for I sinned. I masturbate at least twice a day while I think about having sex with your hot priest who looks like Robert Redford." Right. I think I'll just say I masturbate a lot.

He's stopped in front of the church. He's not going in; he's just staring at the door. Why? Maybe he's thinking about me. *Asshole. Dream on.* He's going in now. Maybe he knew I was following him.

He never turned around. I can't stop thinking about him. I'm obsessed. Because it's forbidden? No, because he's incredible.

I thought I'd really fucked up our first date—at least I saw it as date—but he's agreed to see me again, so it couldn't have gone that badly. If he only knew, though, what I was thinking the whole time we were together, how I wanted to slowly, tortuously, undress him and kiss each part of his body as I revealed it, until he was begging me to go faster. Then I'd rip his clothes off. I'm sure I'm going to hell for thinking it, as well as for everything else I've done. I sure haven't been a saint. But to be fair to me, I haven't been a devil either. I like sex, but I'm not a slut. I've been safe and haven't used guys or lied to them—like they have me. I've always been honest, but that's not what guys in New York want. They don't care. It's all about the quick gratification.

But a priest? Is this some kind of penance for me? I should walk away. But I can't. He's too perfect. I think he's what I've been looking for. Maybe I'll know more after our second "date."

Kell

I paused before opening the door to the church. I sensed him behind me. I'd felt him there since leaving the coffee shop. It could have been creepy, but not in this instance. It felt warm and natural. I purposely didn't turn around the entire walk back. I know if I had turned around and seen him, it would be awkward for both of us. And if I'd turned around and hadn't see him, I would have felt... disappointed. I shouldn't be *feeling* anything close to this, but he'd gotten under my skin. His looks alone could have stopped traffic, and now that I realize that he was the... hunk, (there was no other word for it), on that billboard, my mind was in turmoil. After he told me he was the notorious underwear man, it was all I could do to not picture him naked as he sipped his coffee. I've never felt like I'd betrayed my faith before, until now. My thoughts were not right. I had to quell them, as well as my dormant physical urges. And now, I had all but promised to meet him again. My mind is telling me I have to do this—see where this is leading me, and why. I know I'm deluding myself into thinking this is some kind of test. It's something else. And every instinct I have is telling me that God wants me to explore it.

One Week Ago

Race

"Thanks for coming. I thought I scared you off after the last time."

"Not at all," Kell said. "Thank you for ordering me coffee, perfect for a cool October day. I only had one cup before service. I need another jolt." He smiled at me.

"Father Kell, you're a coffee addict. Isn't there some commandment you're breaking: Thou shalt not imbibe in too much caffeine or something?"

He looked serious. "No, I've scoured the Bible pretty thoroughly now, and there doesn't seem to be anything in there

95

concerning coffee intake. Of course, coffee wasn't discovered until the Middle Ages, so there's that to take into account." He winked.

Ow. Sexy as hell. I need to start rethinking my metaphors. "How about a doughnut or muffin to go with it?" I said, as the waitress approached.

"Why not? Which are you having?"

"Uh, both." I turned to the waitress and she nodded.

"Sounds heavenly." He winked again. "I'll have the same."

"If you do that one more time, I will not be responsible for my actions," I wanted to say. Instead, I said, "What has you so infectiously happy?"

"It's a beautiful day. Service went well. I'm having coffee with a self-proclaimed, good-looking model." Another wink.

Shit. He has to stop that. Every time he does that, it goes straight to my crotch. "You're not going to let me forget that, are you?"

"Should I? Humility is a virtue. Pride—"

"Goeth before a fall," I finished. "I guess I'll have to keep coming to church so you can keep me humble and remind me of my faults."

"I guess you will."

I stared into his eyes and tried to read his mind.

"Give me your hand," he said.

I didn't hesitate. I put my right hand on the table. He grabbed it with both of his. So warm.

"We were placed in each other's path for a reason. God has his ways. It is for us to figure it out. I will not turn away from you or whatever there is between us. I cannot run from myself."

My throat closed. I was going to cry. No man had ever said anything so affective to me. I felt humbled.

He squeezed my hand, sensing I couldn't talk. "It will all work out."

And I knew it would. I had my faith in God. But more... now I had faith in Father Kell.

Present—One Hour Ago

Seamus

"Bless me Father, for I have sinned." I heard from the counter-side of the confessional. "It has been two weeks since my last confession. I need help, some guidance—someone to tell me what to do."

I heard the despair in his voice. I felt a terrible foreboding. "What is troubling you, my son?"

"I have had impure thoughts and feelings for another man." A long pause.

"Go on, my son." Not wanting him to.

"He's a priest, Father." His voice broke. "I'm in love with Father Kell."

My worst fears were realized. This was the man who had brought down Kell, who had made him doubt everything he'd believed in. I needed to be a priest now for this lost soul. "My son, what are you asking of me? He has taken his vows."

"I know." I could hear he was crying. His anguish was heart-breaking. "I don't know what I'm asking. I just need someone to listen. I can't tell my brother. He wouldn't understand. But I need someone to listen. He's so perfect for me in so many ways. He's given me guidance and a purpose, caring, love. I've never had that. I didn't think I could have that—that I deserved it. He looks beyond my face and sees me for who I am. He *cares* about me. Me." It was a plaintive cry. "But, Father, there's more... I slept with him."

Kell

One Day Ago

"Would you like to get something to eat?" Race asked me as the last of the attendants of the five o'clock service passed out the doors. "Or are you busy? I always feel awkward asking you things which are so ordinary for me."

I laughed. "I am man, Race. I eat and sleep and drink like everyone else. You don't have to be careful around me. I did survive our first two coffee chats."

"Don't remind me. I still have nightmares. Does that mean you're hungry?"

"I usually eat after the five o'clock. What did you have in mind?" This was sounding like an actual date, but I was now determined to see where all this led—what God had planned. There was no denying my physical attraction to him, but I was attracted now to the man. His benevolence to do good for others and to want to try to help them was more than admirable. Here was a man who seemed to have it all, yet was so selfless at the same time. He didn't just want to deter the hopefuls from a life as a model, he was insightful enough to realize that people will venture where they are told not to go. He knew people would ignore the "Don't do it" warning. He was giving them the tools, the foreknowledge for what their lives could be like, and when they ran into situations, would then, hopefully, be better off to handle them. I should probably apply this to my work as well.

Race brought me out of my reverie. "I make killer spaghetti. We can walk from here. Garlic bread. Salad. Chianti. Wait, do you drink?"

"Chianti is not my favorite. I'm more an Oregon Pinot Noir man." I have now committed to dinner. At his apartment. Lord, please give me a sign that this is the right thing to do.

Race stared at me. "Argyle—Willamette Valley, Oregon. It's the only red I have at home. How did you know? I only offered chianti because it's expected. I don't like it either, but if you had, I would have gotten some along the way. Argyle. What were the chances? Maybe it's a sign." He laughed.

Maybe it is.

Race

"Well, this is my place." I made a grand arm sweep as we stepped into my spacious living room/dining room. It's what had sold me on it, that and the decent sized kitchen. Nothing like my New York, 600-square-foot shoe box—with no kitchen—for $2100 a month. Roaches optional. New York. What a dump, as the late great Bette Davis once said.

"Nice kitchen," Kell said, scoping out my place.

"Yeah, I like to cook, and now I've got some room to do it. I *can* make a mess. I even had room for my nice little wine rack here." I pointed to the corner of the counter. "Pour you a glass?" I grabbed a bottle off the rack. "In case you're wondering about the full wine rack, I don't drink a lot. I just like the look of a full rack."

"I don't judge." He laughed. God, was he cute when laughed. "And it has a nice aestheticism." He winked. *Shit. Here I go.* That deadly wink. I handed him a glass.

As he roamed around the living room, he said, "I do like what you've done in here. It feels like you. Dark furniture, but you've brightened it up with a yellow throw, and orange and yellow in the pillows. Very nice." He turned to me and raised his glass.

"Thank you." It made me tingle inside, knowing he approved of my taste. I crossed to him and raised my glass. "To my first friend here." I stopped short of clinking his glass. "We are friends, aren't we?"

He looked at me with sincerity. "Yes, Race, we are friends." He clinked my glass and drank. "This is wonderful. I haven't had this for quite a while."

I watched his throat work as he savored the wine and swallowed. My crotch began speaking to me. "Uh, have as much as you'd like. There's lots more."

"I do need to watch it. I don't indulge often, and I want to enjoy this." He sipped and swallowed again. "Can I help with anything? I used to know my way pretty well around a kitchen. I helped my mother cook when I was younger."

"Sure. How about the salad? The fixings are in the fridge."

"Perfect. Will do."

* * *

The meal, the wine, Kell, were all perfect.

Too perfect. This was heading in an impossible direction, but I couldn't help myself. We had finished one bottle of Pinot and were well into the second.

He sat on the sofa. "I have to say, Race, you were right."

"About?" I sat next to him.

"You. You are a good cook. That spaghetti was very different and delicious. I can't believe I ate two big portions. And salad. And four pieces of garlic bread."

"It's my mom's recipe, and I made it yesterday so that the flavors had a chance to really combine. It's called Red Spaghetti, or Spanish Spaghetti. I guess because of the sugar and peppers. I also made my mom's tiramisu, if you think you can squeeze it in."

"You even made tiramisu? How can I refuse?" He finished his glass and reached for the bottle on the coffee table. "I do have a question though," he said to my back, as I proceeded to the kitchen. "How did you know I would come to dinner, since you had made this food in advance?"

Shit. I had hoped he would ignore that. "Prayer?" I gave an awkward smile. "I gave it a shot, figuring if you turned me down, I would have meals for the next couple of days. Although, eating an entire tiramisu would probably mean an extra couple of days in the gym."

He was leaning back on the sofa now, arms spread wide over the back, glass in one hand. Legs spread wide, obviously relaxed and very un-priestly. I couldn't help but notice the way his jeans nicely showed off a great bulge.

He noticed me notice.

I cleared my throat. "I also have a nice tawny port to go with the tiramisu. Of course, the Pinot works, too."

"Ah, port. A heavenly concoction. Or is it decoction? One of those coctions is mixing ingredients, the other comes from boiling something. Whichever coction it is, I would love one."

How many times did he just say cock? Was he getting drunk? I'm a bad man on the road to hell.

"I'll finish this up." He tossed back the rest of his wine. "Bring it on, my friend. I'm not driving and Seamus has got tomorrow's service. But I should probably be going shortly anyway. I'm sure you have things to do."

Was that reluctance in his voice? He was definitely getting toasted. "Here's the tiramisu." I set it down on the table. Aaaand, heeere, is yooour, port," I dragged out and scurried back to the kitchen, then back to the couch.

He scooted closer to me and raised his glass. "Very nice. Real port glasses." His head moved close to mine. "To new beginnings."

We didn't clink glasses. We stared into one another's eyes. Should I? No. I clinked his glass. The moment broken.

"Now, try my tiramisu."

A few minutes later, Kell sat back and said, "That tiramisu was delicious, but not as delicious as this." He raised his almost empty port glass, which I obligingly refilled.

"First, I need your bathroom." He got up a little unsteadily. "All that sugar has gone to my head. I may have to stay a while." He walked down the short hall.

"That's the bedroom," I called out when he switched on the light there. "It's the next door."

"Thanks. Beautiful room, though."

I should have gone with him, but my own head was clouded too, and I didn't want the temptation of having him anywhere near my bedroom. Not yet anyway.

He returned and sat right next to me, our shoulders touching. "Much better. Now, tell me about your ideas for your modeling studio." He picked up his glass.

"I looked around this week and I found a place close to here on the second floor of a fairly new building. And because of the economy, they've had a hard time finding tenants, and the price seems more than reasonable. I can do a six-month or year lease. My only qualm is can I get enough clients. I don't know anyone here."

"You could advertise on the church billboard for starters, and I know many of the owners of businesses in the area. I'm sure they wouldn't mind a few window signs. I'll help you. Who's going to refuse a priest after all?"

Not me. "Thank you, Kell. You've been really positive and supportive. I think I'm going to give it a shot." I leaned in to toast him. He leaned in too.

"I like the smell of your cologne," he said.

"D and G. A perk."

He looked puzzled.

"Dolce and Gabbana—the designers. I didn't just model underwear. I have several bottles. Would you like one?"

"Yes. I think I would, if you're sure. I don't think it's a sin, but it's definitely an indulgence. I'm sure I couldn't afford it. Seamus occasionally wears Old Spice. Usually, though, it's Irish Spring soap. In case you hadn't noticed, he's very Irish. I hope he doesn't get jealous over the "D and G." He laughed, charmingly, of course, and rocked back. *Definitely more than a little tipsy now.*

"Why aren't there aren't any pictures of you around?" he asked.

The quick change of subject threw me. "Uh, I have my portfolio in the bedroom."

"I'd love to see it," he said with a bit too much enthusiasm.

"All right. Follow me." My heart started to beat faster. I'd purposely avoided showing him my bedroom. But he'd asked...

"Yes, a very nice room," he said. "The forest green and gold are perfect. Very rich."

I walked to my dresser and picked up my book. He followed. "This is me."

He zipped open my portfolio and turned to the first page. It was a nice three-quarter shot in jeans and a sport shirt, jacket slung over my shoulder, decent half-smile.

"That's definitely you," he said and turned the page. "And this is your sexy shot?"

I was in very tight jeans, no shirt, arms crossed, sultry look. This photo had pushed my career into high gear and made me a lot of money. It had also prompted designers to want to see me wearing less.

"I guess people thought so. I got quite bit of work after it."

"I can see why," he said guilelessly. "Those jeans don't leave much to the imagination." Maybe not so guilelessly. "I'm sorry. That was inappropriate. I need to stop drinking. And sit down." He backed up a couple of steps and sat on the end of the bed, book in hand.

"Don't worry about it. It's true." I recalled the photographer telling me to make my dick hard, and that if I didn't, he would do it for me. He'd actually threatened me, saying he would get another model and that I wouldn't have been his choice anyway. Bitchy queen. I looked at this photo periodically to remind me of the ugly side of the business—which was most of it.

Kell flipped a page. Oops. My underwear shots. Talk about leaving nothing to the imagination.

Kell was silent.

I sat next to him. "I forgot those were in there. Shit. No, that's a lie. I wanted you to see them." I reached over and slammed the book shut. "I'm an asshole. I'm so sorry. Please... please don't hate me. It's the liquor. No, that's a lie, too. It's you. I'm so confused, Kell." I dropped my head into my hands. I was a fucking mess.

"I could never hate you, Race," he said gently and put a hand on my shoulder. "I'm a priest, remember? We don't hate. Look at me, Race."

I brought my head up and met his tear-filled eyes. "You're a very beautiful man, Race—inside and out. I don't know why God brought us together, but I can't deny my feelings for you either." He seemed very sober now. "They're too strong and feel too right."

He moved his hand to my face and pulled me to him.

When his lips touched mine, the air crackled around us. His lips were soft, supple, gentle, yet held an underlying urgency. It was magical, and I was lost.

His lips parted for me and I eased my tongue between them. He parted them more, and I entered his mouth fully.

My portfolio fell to the floor—silently it seemed—as his other arm came up around my shoulder and we fell back onto the bed completely immersed in the kiss.

His hand played with my back, kneading and squeezing. Exploring. I countered his every move, letting him guide and feel his way. His hands were now on my lower back, pulling me into him. He felt my need as I enjoyed the feeling of his.

He moaned, which forced the same response from me. My desire escalated while his slow exploratory torture continued. I had to hold back. I wanted to ravish him; I wanted him to ravish me. The torment was exquisite. I wanted to scream.

His hands came up and he slowly, excruciatingly, unbuttoned my shirt. Each time his fingers brushed my skin, as more of my chest was revealed, it left a scorch mark. *Shit! I should've worn a pullover.* Then again, I wouldn't have traded this pleasure/agony for anything.

He tugged the shirt from my waist and pushed it back from my shoulders. I watched his eyes stare and take in my bared chest. With his eyes never leaving my torso, he slowly pushed my shirt off my shoulders. It slipped from my arms and fell to the floor. I loved watching him look at me.

He moved back and stared. "Only God could have created something so perfect."

I sucked in my breath to stop my outburst of tears. How had he done that to me with just that simple statement? It was so... honest.

I kept my breath held, as he slowly raised his hands to my chest. It felt like I was waiting to be branded. I could feel the heat coming from his palms. I trembled and my chest involuntarily flexed.

He smiled and whispered, "Magnificent." Both hands settled on my chest.

A lightning bolt shot through me. My body jerked and I groaned loudly. He slowly rubbed his palms back and forth, making my nipples even more erect. They had never been so sensitive. I was frozen with pleasure. I couldn't have moved or breathed if I'd wanted to. And I didn't. I would have visible sear marks from his touch. How could I endure more? He was going to kill me. But what a divine way to go.

Divine. For a moment I almost came to my senses. Kell the priest. Kell the man. A divine man. My man. No matter how this all ended, one thing was certain: there would never be another man for me.

He freely roamed my torso, seemingly fascinated and enrapt. He would sneakily return to my nipples and brush or tweak one, knowing my jerky reaction would follow. I longed to explore him as well, but I needed to hold back and let him go at his own pace.

"I could do this all night," he whispered into my chest, as his tongue came out and licked my nipple.

That did it.

I cried out and clutched his head to my chest, as he sucked hard on my tight nub, a sensation like no other.

He pulled back suddenly. "I'm guessing you like that?" He had a little smirk now. The devil. I liked this side of him. I *loved* this side of him.

My mouth was incapable of speech and I grunted an, "Uh huh."

"Perhaps, I should try the other." And he did.

I clutched at his shirt and wrenched it up. He leaned back and slipped it off, tossing it somewhere.

My turn to stare.

His body was beautiful. Hairless. No, a slight sprinkling of blond fuzz, dusted his chest. He was lean and defined, but not gym-rat defined. Natural—as God had meant. He seemed a divine creation to me. My own body paled in comparison.

He inhaled, thrusting his chest out a little. Inviting. My hands trembled as I brought them up to him. My turn. Finally.

He drew in a breath sharply, while I tried to brand him as he had me. I rubbed and caressed. Glorious. He moaned and writhed at my every movement. I knew what he was feeling. The pent-up energy. We both wanted more.

He sensed the natural progression and slid his hands to my belt, undoing it, next: the button, the zipper. He slid it down, his hand ran the length of me—another teasing scorch. He peeled back my pants and I helped him wriggle them down my thighs, revealing the now very tight, white briefs I wore. His hand cupped me and I thought I was going to explode right then. I pulled back and stood, needing to collect myself. I could barely remove my briefs. He stared intently at my fingers while I slowly slid them down my legs, revealing myself fully to him. I could feel the blood coursing, and an aching throbbing.

He stood. Waiting.

I stared into his eyes. They beckoned to me. I reached out and undid his jeans. I knelt and slid them down his legs, and he stepped out of them, one hand on my shoulder for support. He wore white briefs similar to my own. Purity. Not so much in my case. My eyes were level with his large bulge, also similar to my own. Kell was full of surprises. I breathed heavily and looked up. His eyes locked on mine. His pure and kind countenance had been transformed into one of sexual longing.

I reached for his briefs and held my fingers in the elastic waistband—our eyes still locked. He gave me an almost imperceptible nod and his eyes darkened with desire.

I lowered his briefs, revealing him completely. I reached out and grasped him. He threw his head back, gave a guttural sound, and I began to slowly manipulate him, first with my hands, then with my mouth. He didn't stop me, but rather, encouraged me. His knees began to buckle and I pushed him back on the bed.

"Stop," he pleaded. "No more."

I started to panic.

"Not yet." He sat up. "My turn."

He reached for me now. I rose and stood before him. At last. I had been throbbing for so long, I wasn't sure I could hold back much longer.

He'd obviously been paying close attention to my ministrations of him. He recreated them, then expanded upon them, giving his own special flair. He sensed what would bring me the most pleasure. I was totally lost. Complete euphoria. He was equally lost in pleasuring me, frantic movements followed by slow, bringing me to the edge time and time again, a blissful torture His moans now matched my own. I couldn't discern between the two sounds. The pressure built in me.

When I knew I couldn't last one more moment, I pushed him back and pounced on him. I wanted to give him the full experience. I wanted to give *me* the full experience of *him*. Of us. For nagging at the back of my mind this whole time was the unthinkable thought that this might be the only time I would be with him. *God, please let this not be the biggest mistake of my life. This feels so right, so perfect. How can it be wrong?*

The lights went out. Curious. I'd changed the bulb a couple of days ago. A sign? "We must have blown a fuse," I said while biting his earlobe.

"Or something," he said.

"I have to have you," I added.

"Yes, and I have to have you." His whispered promise in the dark.

Then we gave ourselves totally to one another.

It was heaven.

Seamus

One Hour Ago (con't)

The confessional seemed to close in on me. I couldn't have heard him right. He'd had relations with Kell? I was silent. I needed to process this in my brain. Seamus, you're a priest. You're supposed to help people. Do your job and help this poor boy. He's crying out to you.

"Are you sure?"

"What?" the man said.

You old fool. Of course he's sure. You don't imagine having relations with a priest! "My son, this is a very dire confession. I will make an appointment for you to see Monsignor."

"No, Father. You're Kell's friend. He loves and respects you. I don't want anyone else to know. There has to be something we can do. I think he might love me too." The raw pleading was unbearable.

"Meet me in my office in two hours. I need some time. You do, as well. Use it to pray to the Almighty Father for guidance and forgiveness. He will show us the way. Have faith." I hoped this wasn't a lot of blarney I was spoutin'.

"Thank you, Father. I knew coming to you was the right thing. I'll be there."

As he left the confessional, I stepped out to have a look at him. He plodded to the back of the church, then turned and looked up at the crucifix over the altar. I saw him mumble something and leave. Dear Lord, this man was so strikingly handsome. He looks almost like...

Rory. I thought I'd gotten over those memories a long time ago—that first year in the seminary in Galway.

We'd been young, roommates on our journey to find ourselves and God. He was devilishly handsome. Dark Irish.

I'd lived on a farm all my life. I was so naïve. He was so full of life and piss and vinegar. I followed him blindly. For a while.

Then one night, almost a year to the day of our being there, it happened. Rory said, "All the priests do it or they'd go mad. It's natural. God made us in his image and gave us these feelings and urges, so it has to be all right."

He'd slipped into my bed that night—naked—and began to run his hands over my body. He'd pulled me close and I could feel every part of him. He rubbed and reassured me—but something didn't feel right. He kissed me, and I knew this was not what I wanted. It wasn't God telling me; it was me telling me. I loved him as a brother, but nothing more. I stopped him and said, "Rory, you're my best friend, but I can't do this. It doesn't feel right."

He stopped rubbing me and said, "You're right, Seamus. I guess it's not right for you. It is for me, though. I came here to discover myself, and thanks to you, I have. I love you for it. You're going to be a great priest, Seamus. You have great instincts and conviction. Follow your heart." He kissed me on the cheek and left my bed.

Next day, he was gone. I knew I'd made the right decision. Then why did I feel this emptiness now? I'd just lost my best friend. Could I have handled it better? Could we have stayed friends? It would haunt me for a long time. But I had my path to follow.

Now, here I am, thirty-some–odd years later. There was no one else in the church. I stepped back into the confessional. "Heavenly Father, I ask for your guidance and blessing to do the right thing. Kell is a good priest and a good man. Is it time for him to take a different path? Is this man his path? I know you've chosen me to help these two lost souls. All I'm asking for is some guidance to make the right decision—for both of them. You've tasked with me a difficult one this time. I know you prize love above all, and this seems like the real deal here."

"Follow you heart." I heard from the other side of the confessional.

Rory? "Excuse me, sir. I didn't hear you come in. What was that you said?"

The door on the other side flew open and slammed shut so hard it shook the entire confessional.

I opened my door and said, "Now just hold on there a minute. There's no need to get all fired up and slam—"

No one was there or anywhere. I looked to the same statue of Christ that Kell's young man had been staring at minutes ago. "Thank you, Lord."

Kell

"Please come in, Kell," Seamus said. I entered his office. "We need to talk, my boy."

My stomach knotted with dread. I sat across from him, where I had sat so many times before. Somehow it had all changed.

"Kell," he began. "You know you can come to me with anything. If I had a choice for a son, I could not have chosen a finer one than you. You have become a fine priest, a fine man, and a fine friend. We are none of us perfect. God has made us so. We all have our transgressions and He does not condemn us for them. You have a kind and loving heart and soul. Please, talk to me, Kell."

I could feel the tears start to flow as he spoke. How could I have lied to him? Or at least not told him everything. I knew in my heart he'd understand. Somehow, though, I just couldn't tell him about sleeping with Race. Or more importantly, enjoying every moment of it. I'd never hesitated. It had felt right. It still feels right. *That's* what's wrong.

I looked him squarely in the eyes while I brushed the tears from my cheeks. "I slept with Race."

He nodded. He'd known. "Ah, that's the young man's name."

I was shocked. That was his response? *I* felt like Hester Prynne, but with an 'A' branded on my forehead, or an 'S' for sinner, or an 'L' for liar. I was ashamed. But not for what I'd done. For not owning up to it. For not trusting Seamus. And for not trusting myself.

"I don't feel I've done anything wrong, Seamus... except in not telling you everything. Please forgive me for that. But what I'm doing feels right. God led me to Race, and him to me."

"God works in mysterious ways," he said wryly.

"Seamus, please don't joke." I was irritated now. "This is my life! It's not the gay version of *The Thorn Birds*!"

"Kell, calm down. I'm not joking at all. I've never been more serious. I never ceased to be amazed by how God works. Listen to me. Our God is a loving God and would never turn his back on one of his children because of love. Love is sacred. Above all else, I believe."

My eyes were tearing. I loved this man so dearly.

There was a knock at the door.

"Ah, right on time. Promptness is good, Kell." Seamus winked at me, looking like the cat who swallowed the canary. I stood to get the door for him.

"Sit down, Kell. I'll get it." He went to the door and opened it.

Race.

I sucked in a breath. Our eyes locked.

"Please come in, Race," Seamus said, ushering him in. "Have a seat next to Kell here, whom I believe you've already met."

I was so confused. How did Seamus know Race?

Seamus answered my thought-question for me. "I met Race a couple of hours ago and asked him to come and see me about his little dilemma."

I looked at Race and saw a resigned sadness there, but also... love.

"It seems as though you boys have a similar problem, and I thought by bringing you together we could ferret it out. I've prayed to Our Heavenly Father, as I'm sure you both have, and in his own spectacular way, he answered me. Kell, you have always had my blessing. More importantly, though, I believe you have God's blessing."

"How do you know?" I asked, wanting desperately to believe him.

"I'm goin' ta tell you a little story. When I was in the seminary, I had a best friend, Rory, who I loved very much. But as a friend. I'm afraid he loved me a little more than that. In my naiveté—now I'd call it ignorance—I turned away from him. It hurt him very much, but I didn't know how to properly handle the situation. I lost him. To this very day, I have thought about it and what else I might have done to make it better. His last words to me were, "Follow your heart." I did. I've always hoped that he understood and that he found what he was looking for. I have tried to be the best priest I could be. And, Kell, I've tried to pass on to you everything I've learned. I could not be prouder of you. But now God has thrown you a curve, so to speak."

I was looking at Seamus in a new light. I had to tell him everything. "Seamus, I've only known Race for such a short time. Never in all my years here was I ever even tempted. It just didn't exist for me. I was happy. I can't give it all up. What if it doesn't work out?" I glanced at Race, hoping he wouldn't hate me for my confession, but I had to say it. He had a slight smile on his face. He understood. Of course, he would. He had the same doubts. I honestly did love him.

"There are no guarantees in life, Kell," Seamus said. "Renouncing your vows does not mean renouncing the Church or your beliefs. You can still do great work for this church. They're not going to banish you." He smiled, then brought a fist to his chest. "In your heart, Kell, you know in your heart. And who, do you presume, gave you that heart?" He nodded his head upward a couple of times. "You've only known each other a short while, but who is to say how long you have to know one another? Only you can determine that. I look at the two of you and *know*, without a doubt, that you belong together. I've rarely seen a love so strong between two people. I also believe that together you will do great things. And I trust in you both that you'll let me be a part of these great things."

In spite of the knot in my throat, I managed to say, "I couldn't imagine my life without you, Seamus. How did you get to be so wise?"

"Ha. Wisdom doesn't come with age, I've discovered. It comes with being open and tolerant and ready to see things from many different angles. I have as yet to encounter a situation that was black and white. And I wouldn't use that hackneyed "gray area" phrase, which people are so fond of using when they can't figure out right from wrong. I choose to see each situation as a... a bounty of colors—a vibrant combination—which just needs a little sortin' out.

Sorry for blatherin' so much. I don't where all that came from, but I *do* know what next Sunday's service is goin' to be about. Anything you want to say, Race? I haven't scared you, have I?"

"No, sir... Father... Seamus?" Race stopped.

"Seamus'll do."

"I do have something to say," Race said, taking my hand and looking at me. "I know that I love you, Kell, and want to spend my life with you. My feelings could not be stronger. Everything seems so right when I'm with you. I *know* it's right. I can't help feeling guilty, though, about taking you from your calling."

I gripped his hand tightly. "You haven't *taken* me from anything. You've *given* me the greatest gift—love. I feel whole now. I will stay with the church and also help you in your calling. I felt guided to you. My faith in God is that strong that I know He has guided me to you. Everything about this feels right. You were the missing element of my life. And if a priest falling in love with *you*, an underwear model of all things, isn't enough of a sign—"

"An underwear model?' Seamus broke in.

"Seamus, do you remember that infamous billboard that loomed over the freeway, about a year ago? I think it caused several accidents."

"Kell! Please. Aren't things hard enough?" Race grabbed both of my shoulders to face him.

I stared at him and began a smirk.

Seamus stared at him and raised an eyebrow.

Awareness of the double entendre came into Race's eyes. "Poor choice of words."

Seamus started to chuckle. I joined him. Soon, all three of us were sharing the joke of life's folly.

Seamus stopped laughing abruptly and stared past us. His mouth hung open, his eyes wide. "Rory," he whispered.

Race and I turned around in our chairs to see a blurry image of a young man with such a benevolent smile on his face. I thought it must be some trick of the light. "That's Rory? Is he dead? Is he a ghost?"

"I don't believe so," Seamus said, staring at smiling at the image. "More of an apparition, if you will. I'm glad you're happy, Rory."

The image raised one hand, stretching it toward us, then whispered...

"Follow your heart."

ABOUT THE AUTHOR

Lance Taubold is the recipient of the IBPA Ben Franklin Award for BEST FIRST NON-FICTION for ON TWO FRONTS. He has been an entertainer for 25 years, performing at the MET Opera, on Broadway and on television for 5 years on the soap opera "General Hospital." As a writer he has written for Envy Man magazine, both as a fiction writer and book reviewer. His first novel RIPPER A LOVE STORY was written with author Richard Devin.

Taubold is the author of the gay, paranormal romance series: ZODIAC LOVERS BOOKS 1-5.

Taubold has been a contributor to all of the award-winning NEVER FEAR horror anthologies, the UNCHARTED WORLDS-XENO ENCOUNTERS sci-fi anthology and has romance stories in ROMANTIC TIMES: VEGAS, and THE HAUNTED WEST. His next release is the gay romance, murder mystery MAGIC, MURDER AND MISTLETOE. He is currently writing a paranormal romance series with New York Times Bestselling author Heather Graham.

INVOKE BOOKS

Adventures in all Genres

Exciting Thrillers, Heart-Warming Romance,
Mind-Bending Horror, Sci-Fantasy
and
Educational Non-Fiction

InvokeBooks.com

facebook.com/InvokeBooksPublisher

Feed an Author...

Leave a Review

Never Fear Series

Indie Book Award Winner

New York Times bestselling authors, Heather Graham, F. Paul Wilson, Jon Land, Michael Stackpole, Matthew Costello, William F. Nolan and award-winning, master story tellers bring the best in tales of horror.

Never Fear
Shh... Something's Coming...

Never Fear – Phobias
Everyone Fears Something

Never Fear - Christmas Terrors
He Sees You When You're Sleeping...

Never Fear - The Tarot
Do You Really Want To Know...

Never Fear – Apocalypse
The End is Near...

RT Booklovers Presents: The Haunted West

Written especially for RT Booklovers, best-selling and award-winning authors Diana Gabaldon, Heather Graham, Virginia Henley, Kat Martin, Katherine Neville, Bobbi Smith, Tina Wainscott, Tina DeSalvo and more... take you on a time-traveling, spellbinding journey through America's sprawling West.

The Haunted West, Volume 1

The Haunted West, Volume 2

Romantic Times: Vegas

The Excelsior Hotel and Casino.in Las Vegas is the setting of these magical stories of romance. For decades the towering hotel has been the subject of incredible stories and rumors. Bestselling authors, Christina Skye, Heather Graham, Tina DeSalvo and a story by the Lady of Barrow, Kathryn Falk will take you deep into the heart of those, in the past, present and future... who roam the halls of the Excelsior in search of that perfect love.

Volume 1

Volume 2

Volume 3

Heather Graham's Christmas Treasures

Heather Graham's Haunted Treasures

Presented together for the first time, New York Times Bestselling Author, Heather Graham brings back three out-of-print Christmas classics that are sure to inspire, amaze, and warm your heart.

Heather Graham's Christmas Treasures also available in **Invoke Books Dyslexic Friendly**

New York Times Bestselling Author, Heather Graham brings back three tales of paranormal love and adventure.

The Third Hour

Winner of the USA Best Book Award - Thrillers

The Third Hour is an original spin on the religious-thriller genre, incorporating elements of science fiction along with the religious angle. Its strength lies in this originality, combined with an interesting take on real historical figures, who are made a part of the experiment at the heart of the novel.

Ripper – A Love Story

Prince Edward Albert Victor, The Duke of Clarence is Queen Victoria's favorite grandson and the most eligible bachelor in England. Coren Butler has captured his heart in the perfect Cinderella story. A dream come true. Then the nightmare begins.

Uncharted Worlds: Xeno Encounters

Uncharted Worlds—an exciting new speculative fiction series featuring bestselling and award-winning authors. Ten mind-boggling adventures include tales of ancient aliens, other worlds, and imagined futures.

On Two Fronts

IBPA Silver Medal Best Non-Fiction Award Winner

When two unlikely friends are separated by war, they must learn to cope with the effect it will have on their lives, their futures, and their relationship.

Bad Attitude/Diamond in the Rough

Bad Attitude Meet bad boy, undercover state trooper Reid Cameron. Meet Polly Sweet, the woman who is about to be his downfall. In order to catch a jewel thief, Cameron wants to use Polly's house, and he comes up with a plan, whereby they play at being lovers. But when the first play-acted kiss happens, neither one is ready for the feelings that kiss ignites or for the consequences that ensue.

Has this bad boy finally met his match? How Bad is Too Bad?

Diamond In The Rough-Detective Dan Murdock is on a dangerous stakeout, when advice columnist, Millie Gordon unwittingly shows up on the scene, putting them both in danger. To save her from possibly being shot when the mobsters arrive, Murdock jumps into Millie's car and throws himself over her to protect her, little realizing that the real danger starts when their bodies come together.

Romance and action are the name of the game in this two-in-one duo from bestselling author Doris Parmett

Calendar Girl

Fate, it seems, has derailed destiny... and found a love for all time.
Tina Wainscott weaves a tale you'll not soon forget.

Family

Matthew Costello's widely acclaimed post-apocalyptic thriller, comes to it's amazing conclusion.

Treasures and Pleasures

A Collection of Romantic Novellas from the bestselling author Bobbi Smith.

Shadows in the Big Easy

Bouchercon Presents stories by up and coming Teen Writing Contest winners in this mystery anthology.

Stop Saying Yes – Negotiate!

Stop Saying Yes - Negotiate! is the perfect "on the go" guide for all negotiations. Fortune 500 Companies world-wide send out their teams of negotiators with copies tucked away in briefcases and notebooks... maybe you should too?

Do You Want To Be An Actor?

101 Answers To Your Questions About Breaking Into The Biz from people who know, Casting Directors, Producers, Directors and Agents tell it like it is.

Zodiac Lovers Series

In this series of romantic, gay, paranormal stories tales of love lost, love found, and love to last for eternity will fill your heart with awe and your eyes with tears.

Zodiac Lovers 1: Aquarius, Pisces, Aries

Zodiac Lovers 2: Taurus, Gemini, Cancer

Zodiac Lovers 3: Leo, Virgo, Libra

Zodiac Lovers 4: Scorpio, Sagittarius, Capricorn

Zodiac Lovers 5: Cetus, Ophiuchus